MADE ON EARTH

MADE
ON
EARTH

**What we wear.
Where it comes from.
Where it goes.**

WOLFGANG KORN

A & C BLACK
AN IMPRINT OF BLOOMSBURY
LONDON   NEW DELHI   NEW YORK   SYDNEY

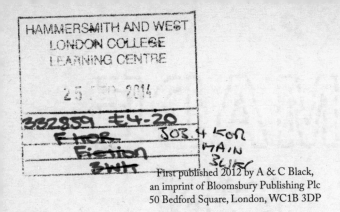

First published 2012 by A & C Black,
an imprint of Bloomsbury Publishing Plc
50 Bedford Square, London, WC1B 3DP

www.bloomsbury.com

Copyright © 2012 A & C Black
Text copyright © 2009 Wolfgang Korn
Translated into English from German by Jen Calleja in 2012
www.jencalleja.com

ISBN 978-1-4081-7391-6

A CIP catalogue for this book is available from the British Library.

This book is produced using paper that is made from wood grown
in managed, sustainable forests. It is natural, renewable and recyclable.
The logging and manufacturing processes conform to the environmental
regulations of the country of origin.

Printed and bound by CPI Group (UK) Ltd, Croydon, CR0 4YY

1 3 5 7 9 10 8 6 4 2

MIX
Paper from
responsible sources
FSC® C020471

Contents

1

How a Fleece Became the Star

It was *not* love at first sight, no way! Bright red fleeces are for young girls, or Liverpool FC fans. They are definitely *not* for tough journalists. When I first saw the fleece, hanging there in the department store, I immediately knew it wasn't for me. I wanted a brown one, though a green one would have been okay, or even blue. But they only had my size in red.

It was late autumn, 2005, and I didn't have the time to look in many shops. I was bogged down in the final phase of writing a book, and I hadn't yet received an advance from my publisher, so I didn't have the money to buy a decent jacket. Winter was approaching, and I was stuck in my office working on the manuscript for eight to ten hours a day. If I didn't want to freeze to my chair, something had to be done.

Two shops and one special offer later, I was the new owner of a bright red fleece. I'd never have guessed that one day I'd write an entire book dedicated to this item of clothing. So how did it come about? Well, in 2007 my publishers wanted me to write a book about globalisation, and although I had had an idea for a long time, I didn't have a main character. To keep them happy, I told them I would come up with a protagonist by Christmas. A character that would take us around the world at breakneck speed, through Asia, Europe and Africa, travelling on ships and sailing across oceans.

Without realising, the days had slipped past and it was already the 21st of December. I needed to come up with a character, and fast! The next day, I hosted an audition to find a star for my book. But the contestants weren't singers or dancers. They were the kind of products that make our lives more convenient and interesting, for example: toasters, computers, MP3 players, vacuum cleaners, bread makers and televisions.

Products like these have done a lot of travelling. But how can we find out where they've been? Their first official destination is the country where they were made. This information can usually be found somewhere on the product, on a sticker, label or stamp. Take my toaster, for example. Where is it from? Hong Kong. My alarm clock? From China. Where did my computer come from? It says, 'Assembled in Taiwan'. Many books written in English are made abroad. My atlas was printed in Slovenia. What about my kettle? This is an exception. It says, 'Made in Germany', which is pretty rare these days! So rare in fact, that the manufacturers have made a big deal about it. However, the country where a product was made is only one step in its life story. Each product's journey starts with the sourcing of raw materials, and inevitably ends with the product being recycled or turned into landfill.

But for now, back to the audition. I had lined up a few interesting products and had already picked a favourite, my laptop. It had an American brand name on it, the processor was made in Germany, and the whole thing was assembled in Taiwan. It sounded like it had been on a very interesting journey. But I really wanted to tell the *whole* story of a product, from sourcing the raw materials to disposal and recycling. If I chose something made out of so many individual parts, I would have too many materials to trace. That would be difficult and time-consuming, and probably boring to read. I needed a different lead for my story. But what?

The next day I was sat in the living room in front of the television. Every year at Christmas, there are lots of news stories about people in need, from the homeless and people who are financially disadvantaged to refugees. One particular story was about African refugees trying to escape to the Canary Islands. Over 60 people were squeezed inside a tiny boat for ten days in the wind and the rain, without any drinking water. Dramatic footage had been recorded by a tourist on camera. The refugees lay on the beach together. There was a quick close-up of a boy wearing a bright red fleece. A red fleece! It was as if a gong had sounded in my head. Was that *my* bright red fleece? I was sure I had put that *exact* same fleece in a clothes-recycling bin where I live just a few months ago. The clothes from that bin, I had just found out, had been sent to West Africa to be sold.

Watching the TV, I thought I recognised a stain I had made on the left hand side of the fleece. Or was it the right? The footage was too poor to tell. I could barely concentrate for the rest of the day. Had that been *my* fleece? Could that have been the same item of clothing I had once owned?

"Do you really believe that it was yours?" asked my girlfriend.

"I've no idea," I admitted.

"Those kinds of fleece body warmers are mass-produced."

"Yes, of course," I replied. "I don't know whether it *really* was my fleece. I have no way to tell it apart from others except by the big stain on the front. Do you want me to pick it out of a line-up?"

"You don't actually want to fly to Tenerife to visit a refugee camp to find a refugee and see if there is a stain on his fleece, do you?" she asked.

"I'm not that stupid. Anyway, I currently lack the necessary funds."

"Thank goodness for that," she replied. "Those people have barely escaped death and you're looking for an old fleece!"

I didn't *really* want to know whether that specific fleece the young refugee was wearing was mine. The fact that it *could* have been mine was more important. After seeing the young man in the red fleece on television, I didn't need to think about what to use as the focus for my book any more. This was much better than a laptop or an alarm clock. The tale of my globe-trotting red fleece would be the perfect way to explain how everything is interconnected.

How did a young man in Africa end up wearing a red fleece that was recycled in Europe? Where was the fleece made? Where did the raw materials come from? Why do people from poorer countries leave their villages to try to get to richer countries? And why are some countries so poor and others so rich in the first place? The answer is ... globalisation.

Examples of Globalisation

Seventy per cent of all cigarette lighters are produced in a single province in China called Wenzhou and then shipped around the world.

When people in America order a tuna fish pizza with extra cheese (or any pizza for that matter) from a local pizza company over the telephone, the order goes through a call centre in India and is then directed through the Internet to the local takeaway in the USA.

Crabs caught in the North Sea are frozen immediately. They then travel by truck through Europe and across the Mediterranean Sea to Morocco (North Africa). The crabs are then processed and brought *back* to Europe.

This may seem crazy to you, but this is how crab sellers in Europe, pizza companies in America and cigarette lighter sellers all over the world save a lot of money. On top of this, the minimum wage in less developed countries is not even a tenth of the minimum wage in industrialised (more developed) countries.

The term 'globalisation' comes from the word 'globe' – a spherical ball that represents planet Earth. In 1983, the American science professor Theodore Levitt tried to find a word to describe how all of the economic activity on the entire planet was connected. Never before had so many people exchanged so many things across the world. Not just objects but also ideas, fashion, music – and above all, *money*. No one was truly isolated from these exchanges, not even rural farmers in the most remote parts of Africa. What we choose to produce and sell has consequences for *everyone* on this planet. Industry is no longer contained within a town, a city or a country, but also spread across the whole globe. This is how 'globalisation' got its name.

24 December 2007

While everyone celebrated around the Christmas tree, I sat at my computer and opened a new document. I tried to remember everything I could about my fleece. The first thing that came to mind was its rich, bright red colour. It was made of a fluffy, warm material, as soft as a rabbit's fur. However fleece fabric is not actually made from natural materials, such as cotton, silk or wool. Fleece fabric is actually made of artificial fibres made from polyethylene – a kind of plastic. And how do we make plastic? Out of petroleum. So where does the story of my fleece really begin? It begins with an order . . .

10 May 2005

The head office of a chain of German department stores is situated near a motorway on the outskirts of Gütersloh, Germany. While the spring sun shines outside, a storm rages in the meeting room. The ordering period for the next season's stock is a stressful time for everyone who works there.

The head of purchasing, Mr Werner Wittkowski, and the new head of marketing, Ms Elfriede Unruh enter the meeting room. They are not getting on well. Mr Wittkowski doesn't want to make any big changes to the purchasing plan, but Ms Unruh wants to shake things up. On the table in front of them is a range of seasonal clothing. There are winter coats made from various materials, heavy denim trousers, woollen knit and polyester jumpers, overcoats and sleeveless body warmers made of corduroy and fleece. There are also piles of clothing brochures advertising hundreds of other garments. Many of the clothing descriptions are written in broken English as most of them come from China and the Far East.

Chinese clothing manufacturers have been flooding European wholesalers and retailers with products that are cheaper than their competitors in Bulgaria, Bangladesh and Turkey for some time. At this particular chain of department stores, many orders for shoes, skiwear and tailored shirts have already been awarded to Chinese manufacturers based on the low prices of their products.

"Next up we have the fleece items," says the director of the company.

Mr Wittkowski hits the brakes on ordering stock from China. "We've *always* ordered our stock from BGI (Bangladesh Garni International) in Bangladesh. Their prices are fair, and the products are good quality."

"At the end of the day, quality in this business is *not* important," interrupts Ms Unruh. "Our customers don't care whether their clothes last five years or one winter. They care about fashion. There is only one trend in the textile industry, cheap, cheaper, *cheapest*. The Chinese manufacturers can make clothes that look as good as named brand products, which are also dirt cheap."

"But we have always ordered our stock from Bangladesh!" protests Mr Whittkowski. "Don't we have a certain obligation to them?"

"No! We can order stock from wherever we like," replies Ms Unruh.

"We have an obligation to our shareholders," the director interrupts. "They want to see growth."

"But what about our customers?" says Mr Wittkowski. "They want a fair price for good quality products. Will the Chinese company keep to the shipping schedules and delivery dates? Will the quality of the stock be consistent and of a high level? Will they use non-toxic dyes? BGI have consistently delivered high quality products at reasonable prices for the past thirteen years."

"That settles it then," replies the director, who has the final say in the matter. "This year, we will continue to order our fleece products from Bangladesh."

The director's PA sends out the orders after lunch. They are signed off by both Mr Wittkowski and Ms Unruh before they are faxed directly to China and Bangladesh. Included in the final order are 1,000 fleece body warmers, made of 100 per cent fleece fabric, with a central zip fastening and pockets, to be supplied in a range of colours including green, blue, grey and brown. Strangely, it seems that bright red fleeces aren't on the list.

2
Can Money Really Buy Everything?

11 August 2005

It's night, and the crude oil that will one day become my fleece is here. But where are we exactly? We are at sea, but close to the coast. Even though it is late in the evening, there is a warm breeze across the water. Around us are burning towers that look like huge, fiery Christmas trees poking up out of the sea. These are platforms where crude oil is drilled for 24 hours a day. The light from the flare stacks can be seen for miles and miles around.

The oil fields here are different to those on land (like in Siberia), and in the north (off the coast of Norway, for example). They are also different to those in Sudan and South America, near Venezuela. These are the oil fields of the Middle East. Here, the land glows like a huge fairground. Aeroplane passengers twist and turn in their seats so they can look down on the bright lights from 10,000 metres above. Many of them will spot a huge spit of land, shaped like an encircled palm tree sticking out of the coast. This man-made island is unmistakable. We are in the Persian Gulf in the sheikhdom of Dubai. Dubai is part of the United Arab Emirates, a country made up of seven individual sheikhdoms that have become super-rich through selling oil. The burning flares and glowing city lights shine all day, every day. When you have a *seemingly* endless supply of natural gas and crude oil, you don't have to worry about your gas and electricity bills.

20 August 2004

It is early in the morning. A drill stands on an oil platform off the coast of Dubai, ready to burrow into a huge underground reservoir of petroleum. The thick black oil explodes up into the sky the moment the drill breaks through the final tightly sealed layer of rock. Over a period of approximately 150 million years, vast amounts of gas have been compressed under immense pressure, resulting in the formation of oil. In the past, oil prospectors would unleash huge fountains of oil that would sometimes catch fire. These days, the oil is safely piped away, day in and day out.

But how is crude oil created? To find out we must go back in time, to between 200 and 900 million years ago. At this point in history, there was only one vast sea, known as the primal ocean, and all the continents were still part of a single connected landmass. Around part of this landmass was an area where the seabed was flat, which we refer to today as the Wadden Sea. It's here that life on Earth began. The first living organisms were blue-green algae; followed by tiny jellyfish-like creatures, the first forms of coral, and *echinoderms* – the forerunners of sea urchins and starfish.

As the Earth's mantle (the planet's rocky outer shell) wasn't as solid as it is today, it could still move around. Over time, increasingly large cracks called basins appeared in the ocean floor. In these basins lived vast amounts of sea creatures that sank to the bottom when they died. There were so many of them that they couldn't all be eaten by other creatures or destroyed by bacteria. Without oxygen they could not rot. Instead they turned the ocean floor into a black marshy expanse. Over thousands and thousands of years, sand and rocks settled on top of this gooey mass. As the dead matter became trapped from all sides, immense pressure built up, which also generated heat. This combination of extreme heat and intense pressure helped to turn the dead organisms into natural gas and crude oil.

Even today, the finer details of how petroleum is created are only just beginning to be understood. In spite of this, for modern humans petroleum is a miracle substance, a form of almost pure energy. If nature hadn't created huge amounts of oil, natural gas and coal millions of years ago, we'd probably all still be travelling by horse and cart and using sailing boats to cross the oceans. Globalisation, as we know it, would not exist. However, these natural energy resources are not equally distributed across the globe. Some countries have very few fossil fuel resources, or none at all, while other countries, like the United Arab Emirates, have vast supplies of fossil fuels such as petroleum.

11 August 2005

Back to the 11 August 2005. The petroleum has been found, drilled for, and pumped out of the ground. Several oil tankers have moored close to the oil platform off the coast of Dubai to collect the oil, including the 187 metre long *Madras*. However, the petroleum is not immediately pumped into the waiting tankers, but runs through a pipeline on the seabed to a storage container on land. At this stage the thick black liquid is a mixture of oil, gas, saltwater and other impurities. It is not yet ready to be transported and sold as it contains too many extra worthless materials.

Once on land, the mixture is moved to a container to be pressurised. The natural gas is extracted and filtered off, which is then used to run Dubai's huge power stations. In another tank the heavy saltwater sinks to the bottom and is pumped away. Using heat, electricity and chemical reactions, the remainder of the water and other waste products are removed. The resulting pure crude oil is now ready to be transported by tankers or through pipelines.

Most tankers drop anchor off-shore while they are waiting for an oil pick-up. The wait can last for several weeks, however the *Madras* only has to wait for 72 hours. In the mornings and evenings when the air is cooler, Captain van der Valt stands on the bridge of the *Madras* watching the coastline through his binoculars for hours on end. Every time he sails to Dubai, he feels like he's arrived on the set of a science-fiction film. The top floors of the skyscrapers glow blue and look like giant, alien heads. Other constructions look like docking stations for missiles, although in reality they are brightly lit building sites surrounded by cranes, the birthplaces of future skyscrapers.

14 August 2005

The opportunity for the *Madras* to dock in the Jebel Ali Port comes at sunrise. Dubai's new harbour, which was created to cater to huge cargo ships, is the largest port in the Middle East. Due to the enormous size of oil tankers however, oil shipments have to be exchanged outside of the main harbour. At about 8:00am in the morning the *Madras* enters the filling station. Three massive hoses are lowered by crane onto the deck of the ship and positioned so that the crude oil can be pumped into the ship's storage tanks. It takes well over a day for the tanker to be filled.

While this is happening, Sadek, an immigrant from India, is finishing breakfast with his housemates in a simple apartment on the outskirts of Dubai. Sadek and his friends are part of the foreign workforce that make up more than three quarters of Dubai's population, and who undertake almost all of the manual labour in the city. Immigrants like Sadek work on oil rigs and on building sites, they cook and wait on tables in restaurants, and they work in the homes of some of the wealthiest people in Dubai. They take care of private and public gardens, clean the streets and drive taxis. These workers earn around £100 to £120 pounds a month. They send most of this money home to their families, who must survive on this source of income alone. Immigrant workers can often earn more than double the wages they could in their homeland working as skyscraper construction managers, vets on camel farms or engineers on the drilling platforms.

Sadek, however, earns his money by loading and unloading small boats in the old port. The old port is situated in an estuary that extends almost ten kilometres into the heart of Dubai. The estuary has served as a natural harbour for centuries, and throughout this time the dhows, the traditional wooden boats of the Arabian Gulf, have anchored here. Forty years ago Dubai was just a small trading post. Only a few of the houses were made of stone, and most were built from clay and had roofs made of palm fronds. Although the town has changed completely in the last few decades, the dhows still transport almost all trade goods in the Persian Gulf, including car tyres, non-perishable goods and electrical supplies from the Far East. While Sadek and his colleagues move crate after crate onto land in the heat, an Arabian dhow captain watches and grumbles to himself. But the dock-workers are happy because the port is busy. Sometimes they have to sit for hours in the shade waiting for boats to come in.

When Captain van der Valt first sailed a ship to Dubai in 1990, the eight-lane Sheikh Zayed road which runs parallel to the coast had just been built. Many foreigners mocked the so-called 'Grand Boulevard of Dubai', as the road ran through undeveloped wasteland. Now however, the highway is surrounded by high-rise offices, hotels and apartment complexes. Construction goes on uninterrupted day and night. Today in Dubai, over 200 skyscrapers have been built, surpassing the number in Hong Kong and New York City. Only the smaller high-rises are simple in design and construction. The large skyscrapers revel in how elaborate and complicated they are; the luxury Burj al-Arab Hotel for example, looks like an upturned ship, while the Jumeirah Beach Hotel looks like an enormous slide. These buildings, however, pale in comparison to the Burj Khalifa. It is currently the tallest structure in the world, measuring 829.84 metres high. The Burj Khalifa has 160 floors, with a hotel at the bottom, a viewing platform at the top, and offices and luxury apartments in the middle.

The 'Miracle of the Persian Gulf': Dubai

Dubai is one of seven small sheikhdoms in the middle of the Persian Gulf, which together make up the United Arab Emirates (UAE or Emirates, for short). The country is hailed as the 'Miracle of the Persian Gulf'. While bloody conflicts raged on around it, Dubai became an oasis of peace and economic growth, where people from different races and religions could live side by side. Thanks to its rich oil supplies and shrewd economic policy, Dubai has become one of the 'winners' of globalisation. It is, per person, one of the richest countries in the world. In order to show the world just how rich the Emirates are, they have built the highest skyscrapers, the largest man-made islands, and are in the process of building the world's largest theme park (Dubailand).

Despite its wealth however, three quarters of Dubai's population are not actually made up of citizens of the United Arab Emirates, but poorly paid immigrants with temporary work permits.

What the Emirates lack, however, is a good supply of natural drinking water. In spite of this, they use more than a million cubic metres of water a day. Only the USA and Canada use more water per person per day. The UAE's fresh water supply comes from desalination plants, which are powered by locally sourced natural gas and petroleum. The Arabians in the Gulf still have plenty of these fossil fuels available, but they will, eventually, run out. This is the reason why the government sees the country's future in trade, finance, retail and tourism. Hotels and parks attract tourists, and man-made islands, luxury apartments and docks for private yachts attract wealthy immigrants. In addition to expanding the country's aeroplane fleet, the government is also building two new airport terminals, one for passengers and one for cargo.

14 August 2005

By the evening, the *Madras* is only a third full. The filling process takes between 36 and 40 hours. A tanker like the

Madras can hold around a million barrels of crude oil – that's around 159 million litres. The loading and unloading of the six tanks inside the ship is coordinated by Portuguese first mate and boarding engineer, Raul. A warning system of sensors controlled by a high-tech computer program makes sure that the tanks are filled evenly. If one section becomes overloaded, the hull could buckle like an empty shoebox.

During the filling process, the oil company is in frequent contact over the radio. They want to know exactly how everything is going. For them, time *is* money. It costs the oil company $50,000 US dollars a day to rent the tanker. That is a cost of at least $75,000 US dollars *before* the oil is even on board! Every hour costs them another $2,080 dollars. The oil company tries to put pressure on the crew to speed up the filling process, but Captain van der Valt and his crew are experienced sailors and don't get flustered easily.

15 August 2005

For most of the Arabians living in the Gulf, driving their expensive cars along the Sheikh Zayed road to the mosque on a Friday, there is not a single oil rig or refinery in sight. They don't have to think about the oil reserves – just knowing they are there is enough. If you're the son of a citizen of Dubai, like 13-year-old Mohammed, you don't have to worry about oil or money. Many Arabians in the Gulf make a living either from rent – as landlords for the shops and apartments, or from shares and investments. Others sit on the board of directors for local and international companies (in Dubai, international companies cannot undertake business without a local contact). Mohammed's father is one of the directors of a company that runs Dubai's oil treatment plant and operates the oil distribution terminal. Once or twice a day he looks over the paperwork and signs a few documents – the rest takes care of itself.

In some cases in Dubai, the interest rates, financial rewards and levels of business responsibility awarded to each citizen are closely linked to their family name. The closer a citizen's family is to the 'tribes' of Dubai's ruling family, the bigger the financial rewards. A tribe is made up of all the members of a particular family. The tribe arranges everything for its members throughout their lives. Mohammed is part of this tribe culture. He attends school in the mornings, plus twice weekly he attends Qur'an school in the afternoons. In a year he will be sent to a boarding school in Switzerland.

At present however, every Friday Mohammed goes to the mosque in Dubai and then has a meal with his family. He may only speak if he is spoken to – this is an unwritten law in Arabian countries. The family meal follows strict traditional rules. The men wear long white robes known as kandura and guthra (headscarves) on their heads. They keep to themselves, while the women and young children eat in a separate group. The food is laid out on a huge, fine Persian carpet. There are countless small sharing dishes to start the meal: marinated aubergines, olives, rich hummus, toasted sesame seeds, marinated garlic, cheese, and a range of delicious sauces. The traditional main dishes are grilled lamb kebabs, roasted lamb, and marinated lamb in a rich sauce, served with a mountain of rice.

Traditionally, people only eat using their right hand. If someone put their left hand in the communal rice, the other diners would recoil in disgust. This is because hundreds of years ago, the nomadic tribes of the Gulf used their left hands to wipe themselves after going to the toilet. Even though nowadays people can afford bathroom suites with inbuilt showers, this knowledge from the past has left a lasting impression: you *only* eat with your right hand.

It could be said the citizens of Dubai, like other Arabians in the Gulf, are torn between the present and the past. They have built the most modern city of the 21st century. They drive fast cars, wear expensive rings and watches and play golf. They travel to New York, London and Munich with huge entourages and stay in luxurious hotels. But at the same time, they don't want to be separated from their traditional way of life.

After dinner the men sit and smoke shisha (flavoured

tobacco) and drink strong tea or coffee. The head of the tribe asks, "Mohammed, have you thought about where you would like to study in the long term? Have you picked a good university in America or England yet?"

Mohammed blushes and looks down at the floor. He doesn't want to lie, but he knows that telling the truth just isn't worth the hassle. His father answers for him, "If it was up to Mohammed, he would become an ice-hockey player!"

All the men in the room laugh. Unfortunately for Mohammed, even the citizens of one of the richest countries in the world can't always do what they want. The fathers and the heads of the tribes always have the last word. The leader of Mohammed's family tribe sets down his tea glass, folds his hands and looks at Mohammed. "If we all followed our dreams, we would all be racing drivers, poker players and camel jockeys!" he says. "But then Dubai would only have a few skyscrapers, and they would all belong to foreign investors. We are strongest when we work together. Allah has chosen a role for each of our family members. Dubai's oil will soon run out. The money we have made has been cleverly invested, but what we are missing, young man, is *knowledge*. How do you build a skyscraper? How do you create a mobile phone network and boost the signal to improve reception? How do you manage a hotel or a theme park with over a thousand employees? To answer all of these questions we still need outside help, and this is why our cleverest sons have to become engineers and managers. When I speak of our clever sons, I mean *you* Mohammed!"

Mohammed looks at the floor and lets his mind wander – his thoughts are of ice hockey, just as they are at every Friday family dinner. Finally, it's time for him to leave. His chauffeur drives him to the winter sports centre, which includes an enormous snow park with a real snow ski slope. When you have vast amounts of oil and gas at your disposal, the cost of refrigeration isn't a problem. Mohammed waits for his teammates in the changing rooms. He pulls on his ice hockey shirt and puts on his skates – both were 'Made in the USA'. On the ice rink, his coach is already carving out a route across the ice. He smacks the puck into the left-hand corner of the goal. Mohammed's trainer is Canadian and used to play ice hockey professionally in Canada. How much ex-professionals get paid to teach young people ice hockey in Dubai is a state secret. If you want to know more about winter sports in Dubai, visit **www.skidxb.com**.

Even though Mohammed is wearing a padded ice hockey shirt he feels a little chilly. A fleece body warmer would come in handy right now. He obviously wouldn't wear one like mine though: his would be a designer fleece. Not that it matters anyway though. My fleece is not even close to being finished. In fact, its journey has only just begun.

3

Oil Tankers: The Whipping Boys of Globalisation

16 August 2005

It's morning at Jebel Ali Port. While Sadek cycles to work at Dubai's old port and Mohammed walks to school, the *Madras* finally leaves Dubai. There is barely a metre between the heavily loaded ship and the seabed, so the tanker moves cautiously until it enters deeper water. The raw materials for my fleece are finally on their way to Chittagong, Bangladesh, at a speed of exactly 15 knots (around 24 kilometres an hour). The tanker's speed is closely regulated by the oil company, which pays for the fuel used to run the ship.

Captain van der Valt cannot relax until the *Madras* has sailed through the treacherous waters of the Persian Gulf and the Strait of Hormuz. He must stay on the bridge to navigate regardless of how long the journey takes, which can be up to 16 hours. The sea is shallow and the Gulf is narrow, and the many tankers and ships sailing through the bay have to pass in extremely close proximity with one another. The coast of the strictly Islamic country of Iran stretches out behind the *Madras*. Boats patrol its territory vigilantly.

After almost 150 kilometres the *Madras* reaches the Strait of Hormuz, where the shipping lane is only 100 metres wide. Thankfully, there is no queue of tankers waiting to pass through the strait, so the *Madras* can sail on without stopping. After almost 13 hours, the *Madras* finally reaches the Oman Gulf, which opens out onto the Indian Ocean. Finally Captain van der Valt can leave the bridge, go to bed and sleep.

The rest of the tanker's route is simple. It will sail across the Indian Ocean to the most southern point of India, and from there it will head in the direction of Bengal. For most of this 4,500 kilometre stretch of sailing, the helmsman will have only one instruction: steady as she goes. The rest of the crew have to focus on keeping the motor running at its optimum capacity and on the general state of the tanker and its cargo. Carrying 180,000 tonnes of crude oil can be likened to ferrying around a sleeping, irritable dragon. In order to prevent rough seas from causing the oil to slosh around dangerously inside the ship, the loading space is divided into six individual tanks, which are supported with steel beams. If the interior of the tanker was simply one huge hollow space, the pressure of the seawater from outside would crush the ship like a shoebox as soon as it was emptied.

20 August 2005

The monitoring of the ship and its cargo takes place from the control room at the back of the ship. This means that Dutch Captain van der Valt, Portuguese first mate and boarding engineer Raul Jorges and the 21 Filipino crew members spend their entire journey in one small area at the rear of the ship.

Only one crew member regularly ventures out onto the deck: Raul, the first mate. In order to stay fit, he spends his free time using the 200 metre steel giant as a running track, jogging past pipes, thick anchor chains, hose pumps and huge vents. Raul only has to do 30 laps of the deck to run 12 kilometres, which he tries to do daily. Here in the tropics however, the temperature reaches 30° Celsius by mid-morning, and Raul breaks into a sweat so quickly that he usually only runs about half that distance. After all, he needs to hold back some energy for his daily tasks on the ship and for his favourite hobby, chatting online.

Super Tankers

The 194 metre long *Madras* is a *LR2* (*Large Range 2*) tanker, built for covering medium stretches of water and entering shallow harbours. She can hold around 125,000 tonnes of crude oil or other liquids and has a 125,000 deadweight tonnage. (The deadweight tonnage is the maximum possible weight a ship can safely carry, and is often abbreviated to DWT).

Super tankers are categorised as *VLCC*'s (*Very Large Crude Carriers*, which can carry over 200,000 DWT) and *ULCC*'s (*Ultra Large Crude Carriers*, which can carry over 300,000 DWT). These days most super tankers are between 310 and 350 metres long, have a capacity of up to 350,000 DWT, and are run by 30 to 40 crew members.

But what *is* 350,000 DWT? A super tanker in the *ULCC* class can hold two million barrels, or 318 million litres, of crude oil. That is the equivalent of 17,000 road tankers.

Super tankers in excess of 400 metres have been built, but they are difficult to control and can only use a limited number of shipping routes due to their enormous size. Even super tankers of 300 to 350 metres in length can only dock at a few harbours, due to the depth of their hulls.

On board the *Madras*, first mate Raul thinks the Internet is an amazing invention. He spends a huge amount of his free time on board the ship discussing his views online with people all over the world. He shares his extensive knowledge about the oil industry, machinery and shipping routes on online forums. He also uses the Internet to let off steam. It really annoys Raul that no one likes tanker ships. Admittedly, oil tankers aren't beautiful; in fact they're pretty ugly. But oil tankers are an integral tool for the whole of the human race. Super tankers are also the largest steel constructions ever built by humans. At up to 400 metres in length, many are larger than the Eiffel Tower in Paris, which is only 320 metres high. Furthermore, the Eiffel Tower is made up of lots of small pieces to form a large steel frame. The body of a tanker, on the other hand, is made of vast sheets of welded steel. A double-thick exterior wall also protects newer tankers. From 2015 this will be the official standard for all tankers worldwide.

In spite of this, when most people hear the word 'super tanker', they immediately think of accidents, environmental catastrophes and ruined beaches. Raul thinks this is hugely unfair. Firstly, accidents resulting in environmental catastrophes are incredibly rare, and secondly, it is almost *never* the fault of those who work aboard the tankers when such accidents do occur. The blame usually rests with tanker owners who refuse to remove older, less seaworthy vessels from service. Oil consumers who want their petrol to be as cheap as possible, but don't want to know *how* the oil products they use are transported, can also be held accountable. Cost cutting has consequences.

These days, a lot of oil is transported through pipelines, such as the pipeline from Siberia to Western Europe. But oil tankers are still at the heart of the crude oil chain. Online, people take a stab in the dark when Raul asks them how many tankers are shipping oil at any one time. Most people imagine it is 1,000 or less. Others are convinced it is 2,000 or 3,000 ships. In actual fact, the number is closer to 7,000 ships at any one time. But even 7,000 ships are not enough to keep up with the world's growing demand for oil.

Even the tanker operators themselves don't seem to like oil tankers, which is resulting in fewer being built. Within the next few years, there will be a shortage of tankers in the oil transport industry. If there is a shortage of tankers, then older, less seaworthy tankers will have to remain in service for longer, which will increase the chances of some kind of accident, resulting in an oil catastrophe. This will give tankers an even worse reputation, and so the cycle goes on . . .

Could it really be that *everyone* in the world hates oil

tankers? Apparently not. Raul has managed to find a small group of tanker fans online. Like train spotters, there are a few hardcore enthusiasts who spend their spare time ambushing tanker ships in harbours and straits so they can take photographs of them and post them online. Images and information on just about every kind of tanker ship are shared and discussed on the tanker fans' forum. On a page called, 'Mystery Tankers', users are quizzed for information about any tankers the fans have so far been unable to identify.

Raul also takes part in online chats about energy and environmental issues. These cover many hotly debated topics, especially the rapidly rising use of oil. Worldwide, we currently use around 85 million barrels of oil *a day*. A barrel is around 159 litres. Humans use 13,515,000,000 (13 billion, 515 million) litres of oil each day, which means that over the course of a year we use the almost unimaginable sum of 4,932,975,000,000 litres, or in words: 4 trillion, 932 billion, 975 million litres. Three quarters of this total is burnt by industrialised Western nations in the form of petrol, diesel and aircraft fuel. Over the past few years, an increasing number of countries have caught up (and even surpassed) the West in terms of oil consumption. India and China are the most noteworthy, as their energy use has risen astronomically in the last few years, but countries on the outskirts of Europe like Ireland and Poland, or Raul's homeland Portugal, are also increasing their energy consumption. All in all, the world's energy use will rise by 50 per cent over the next 20 years. This will mean that more and more goods will be sent around the world, more and more people will travel to far away countries, and more and more cars, ships and aeroplanes will need fuel.

Raul is a shining example of how things could be different. At home he has installed solar panels on the roof of his house. He has also invested some of his savings in Portugal's first wind farm, and is always pleased to see the huge wind turbines turning on the North Atlantic coast. He understands however, that the change from burning fossil fuels to using renewable energy sources will not happen overnight. There are many renewable energy sources available: hydroelectric and wind power, solar power and bio gas. But at the current uptake rate, these sources won't be able to cover even a quarter of the world's energy needs in 20 years time.

Raul is also frustrated by other nonsensical ideas about oil tankers that he comes across in online environmental chatrooms. For example, the comment, "The distance oil tankers have to travel to transport oil is the reason petrol is so expensive."

"This is not true!" Raul explains to other users in the

chatroom. "Renting a super tanker costs anywhere up to $80,000 US dollars a day, which means in comparison to the price of oil, transport barely costs anything. If, for example, we were carrying 1.5 million barrels of oil (240 million litres) over a long distance, say 10,000 kilometres, it would take approximately twenty days for the journey there and back." Raul works out the calculations in his head. "Twenty days at $80,000 dollars is a total tanker rental cost of $1.6 million dollars, divided by the cargo of 240 million litres of oil, equals a transport cost of approximately $0.0066 dollars per litre! Transportation costs less than half of one per cent of the sale price of a litre of oil."

At the same time, someone else involved in the discussion asks the most frequently asked question in the chatroom, "How long will oil supplies last, in light of the world's increasing demand for energy?"

Someone called Warner replies, "The government is lying to us all. The oil has almost run out and soon the world will be left in darkness."

Raul won't stand for this kind of scaremongering. "There are plenty of reserves left for the foreseeable future, plus oil extraction technology has recently made great advances," Raul replies. "Fields that were once overlooked or at great depths can now be found and exploited. At the moment we know of at least 42,000 oil fields, many of which have not yet been explored."

"That's completely wrong," Warner says. "The largest oil fields are all but used up. And only 300 of these 42,000 fields are economically viable. There will be a dramatic oil shortage within a decade!"

"No," Raul disagrees. "In ten years time, oil processing will have developed in ways that are currently too expensive to be economically viable. For example, at the moment, if oil is mixed with sand, we don't process it, as it is too expensive. The bigger question is *when* will oil production become so expensive that it is no longer *worth* producing? When will petrol be too expensive for the average car driver? The production of cost-effective energy depends not only on oil, but also on the discovery of other energy sources *and* the needs of the consumer. In a recent survey, 80 per cent of European car drivers stated that they would cut down their car use if petrol prices continued to increase."

Raul shuts down his computer. While leaving his room and taking the stairs to the ship's bridge, he goes over the debate in his head. He is amazed by the lack of public knowledge about fossil fuels and the global energy supply. Despite all the modern technology used in the oil industry; GPS systems that can pinpoint the whereabouts of a ship to the metre and instruments that can measure crude oil to the litre, when it comes to questions about the worldwide energy supply, the general public really have no idea.

22 August 2005

When the *Madras* reaches the Bay of Bengal two days later, it sails past more oil platforms rising out of the water. Bangladesh actually has its own offshore oil fields, and the oil is transported through a pipeline to the city of Chittagong. In spite of this, Bangladesh still needs to import oil. Bangladeshi oil needs to be blended with oil from the United Arab Emirates in order to meet Bangladesh's energy needs. One oil is too sulphurous, the other too viscous (thick and sticky). Mixing the two together creates the perfect blend.

The water in the Bay of Bengal is slowly turning brown, but not from contamination with crude oil. It is from India's great rivers bringing their brown waters deep into the bay. Bangladesh is located in the centre of three large rivers, the Ganges, the Brahmaputra and the Meghna. Over centuries, the place where the three rivers meet has forced the silt they carry to build up and extend the land further and further out to sea. This land is very fertile, but liable to flooding and hurricanes. Chittagong is Bangladesh's only sea harbour and is situated east of the river delta on the Karnaphuli River.

Long before the *Madras* reaches the harbour, it sails past many much older ships. They are obsolete oil tankers, cargo ships and ferries waiting to be dismantled on Chittagong's beach. In the ship breaking zone, most of the boats are taken apart by hand. Last year, Captain van der Valt wanted to take a closer look at the area, and took a taxi down to the beach. "We used to swim here," the taxi driver told him. Nowadays, the whole beach is covered in black, sticky oil.

Half submerged and half on land, the huge ships lie around like beached whales. A cargo ship is having its bow cut away, while the stern of a tanker lies next to it, the rest of its superstructure remaining in the water. There is nowhere to dock, and no wharf where the back-ends of ships can be placed above the water line. A huge crane moves around, swaying to and fro, transporting heavy pieces of iron. Everything else is done by hand using basic hand tools, welding irons, screwdrivers and chisels. The workers look very small next to these vast ships, and very vulnerable.

"A lot of accidents happen here," one of the workers told Captain van der Valt. "But our employers just don't want to know." Oil and grease from the ships' machinery and tanks isn't pumped out into a collecting reservoir. Instead, it is left on the beach.

The city of Chittagong is not directly on the beach, but is

further inland on a wide river called the Karnaphuli. The river, however, is only six metres deep, which is why Chittagong's oil harbour is at the mouth of the river, at the end of a long spit of land, far out to sea. As soon as the *Madras* arrives at the oil harbour, the crude oil is pumped out of the ship into huge tanks. The tanks are already half full with crude oil from the Bangladeshi oil reservoirs. The combination of the two oils will be better for processing. After the *Madras* has been emptied, its tanks are thoroughly washed out with water. Then the ship goes through a rigorous safety check. A team of experts climb on board and swarm all over the ship, checking the electronics, pipes and valves. They even climb into the oil tanks. Crude oil, saltwater and oxygen irritate the walls of the ship. Although the walls are always sprayed with a protective coating, the combination of oil, saltwater and oxygen will eventually burn through and attack the metal below, making it rust. Only once the experts have worked through their entire list can the ship leave. Time is of the essence, as always. After all, renting the *Madras* costs $50,000 US dollars a day . . .

4

A General Strike in Chittagong: Bangladesh Hangs By a Thread

23/24 August 2005

It's late at night in one of the slums of Chittagong. In the darkness, Mohmin and his young neighbour Kholil are discussing strike demands with their colleagues. The electricity network is down again so they have to finish their banner, made from a bed sheet and two poles, by the light of a petrol lamp. They are still undecided about what to write on the banner. They want better pay, that's for certain . . .

Mohmin works at the polyester factory, and Kholil works at the plastic recycling plant. They are sick of the terrible pay. They work until they drop and yet their families still have to live in the slum districts. Plus there is the problem of safety in the workplace. Mohmin knows what he's talking about. He used to work at the oil refinery near the harbour. The refinery, which produces petrol, heating oil, chemicals and asphalt from crude oil, could be mistaken for some kind of industrial museum, not a modern oil refinery. It is actually built from parts of an old industrial unit from the United Kingdom. Forty or fifty years ago, English chemical workers used these very same machines. But then the unit was put out of action. It was too old, too unproductive and too dangerous to pass health and safety laws in England. But it was not too dangerous for the chemical workers of Bangladesh. The refinery workers spend day and night walking through a labyrinth of pipes and metal tanks, wearing only loincloths and putting up with a combination of heat, noise and vile smells. There are no health and safety regulations and no protective clothing.

It's not surprising that Mohmin was overcome by toxic fumes which made him so sick he had to go to hospital. By the time he was back on his feet, his job had been given to someone else. Factory owners in Bangladesh don't have to give their workers sick pay. They simply replace them. There are hundreds more desperate people looking for work who are willing to take their place. Mohmin and his colleagues are keen to make a point about safety, but the line, "Improve Safety in Dangerous Workplaces!" doesn't sound quite strong enough. In the end, Kholil, the only one of them who can write properly, writes: "Thirty Per Cent More Now!" on the banner instead.

Bangladesh: a Country in a Precarious Situation

Bangladesh, at 144,000 square kilometres in size, is not even half the size of Germany (357,000 square kilometres), yet has over 140 million inhabitants. Germany, by contrast, only has a population of 82 million people. Bangladesh is the most densely populated country on the planet, with around 1,000 people living in every square kilometre. Germany, by comparison, only has 232 inhabitants per square kilometre. In Bangladesh, 70 per cent of the population live off of the land. Because of the high population density, farmers must produce crops that give the best possible yields using the smallest possible amount of space. This is why Bangladeshi farmers don't produce cotton, but do grow a lot of rice.

The tropical temperatures don't last all year round in Bangladesh. For almost half the year nothing can be grown. In March, April and October, tropical hurricanes and storms batter the country, and June to September is monsoon season. High winds blow blankets of cloud across the country and there's almost non-stop heavy rainfall. Most of Bangladesh is made up of marshland, intersected by three large rivers. During the monsoon, as much water as is contained in all the rivers in Europe flows through these three rivers. When the water is pushed back into the river delta by storms at sea, this causes major flooding.

At the moment, Bangladesh has no way to prevent this from happening, and every year, water floods the fields. Each year the flooding gets worse because of the rising sea levels caused by global warming. In 2004, the homes of 34 million Bangladeshis – almost a quarter of the population – were flooded. Richer countries can protect themselves with sea walls and high dams, but there are no protective measures available in Bangladesh. Even when funding is received in order to build dams, the government is so corrupt and badly run that the money is almost always spent elsewhere. By the year 2050, about a sixth of the country will be permanently underwater. Around 20 million people will loose their homes and livelihoods forever.

24 August 2005

It is now morning. Mohmin and Kholil don't head towards the harbour for work as usual, but instead walk into town, to the main street in front of the train station. More and more workers assemble there. Some of them are wearing helmets and are armed with sticks. On the banners and placards that many of them are holding are messages about pay, safety and job security:

"Down with corporations!"
"Down with the government!"
"GENERAL STRIKE!"

The signs are written in Bengali and also in English so that foreign reporters and people watching the news in other countries will understand them. The assembled workers are calling for a general strike. This is when all workers and employees across the whole city refuse to work. Buses, ships and trucks come to a standstill, factories stop running and shops are closed. There have been three strikes already in Chittagong this year. When a general strike happens in Chittagong, the whole country shuts down, as almost everything Bangladesh produces is shipped out of Chittagong harbour. When the harbour and the refinery stop working, all manufacturing *has* to stop. This time, the government has had enough, and its response is aggressive. The police and the army are mobilised and sent to the harbour, the oil refinery and the large crossroads in the centre of town. However, the police and army presence isn't enough to silence the workers and strike leaders. They form a group and start walking down Station Road. They're heading for the Dhaka Trunk Road that leads to the harbour.

Kholil and Mohmin hold their home-made banner high, but they only make it a few hundred metres down the road. The police have blocked off the road with riot vans and water canons. In front of them are two rows of police wearing helmets, carrying shields and heavy batons. There's a sudden popping noise. Are the police firing at them? The strike leaders try to calm the crowd. "Don't panic!" they cry. "It's only tear gas! Cover your faces! Don't rub it into your eyes!" Then the police rush forward. They use their shields to shove aside anyone who's in their way and brutally hit the demonstrators with their batons. Kholil has never been so scared in his entire life. He drops the banner, flees down a side street and runs away. Mohmin, on the other hand, won't let the banner go. He is surrounded by police trying to tear it out of his hands, but with great determination, he holds on. Moments later he is hit over the head with a baton, and two police officers drag him into a riot van. While sirens wail outside, the harbour's oil refinery is put back into action, under police supervision.

Meanwhile, our mixture of crude oil, delivered a few days

ago, is being pumped through the long pipelines of the refinery. In this labyrinth of tunnels, oil containers and machines steam, hiss and rattle. The first process to refine oil is to heat the crude oil to 400° Celsius in a 50 metre high cylinder, known as a 'distillation column'. Here, the different components that make up crude oil separate: gases and light petrol evaporate and rise upwards, while tar and lubricating oil sink to the bottom. Somewhere in the middle is coal, which is made of carbon, and just below that is ethylene, the raw material for many kinds of plastic. These basic components are then separated out, and moved on for the second stage of processing.

The ethylene is combined with a catalyst – the reactive metal antimony – under high pressure, and then heated to 240° Celsius. During this process, the individual ethylene molecules gain the ability to bond into a single mass. This creates polyethylene, a substance made up of a seemingly endless molecule chain. No other substance is so stable and yet so malleable. At the bottom of the machine in which this process takes place are six holes. The white-grey polyethylene is squeezed out of the holes in pencil-thick strings, almost like toothpaste being squeezed out of a tube. The threads of polyethylene are then cut into smaller segments and cooled. These hazelnut size pieces are called 'granules' and are the raw material for a huge range of products. Polyethylene is a truly magical substance. At 120° Celsius it becomes a liquid, and can either be formed into the desired shape or pressed into thin sheets. Polyethylene and similar man-made substances are the foundations for our globalised, consumer-driven world. These materials are used to make carrier bags, packaging, mobile phone covers, iPods and laptops. Various medications and colours used in paint and foods also contain components derived from crude oil. Most polyethylene however, is used for packaging. In a globalised world where products travel long distances between the manufacturer and the consumer, packaging is essential. There's packaging for packaging. There's even packaging for *used* packaging – here in Germany we have special yellow rubbish bags for plastic recycling.

In many parts of the world, people open their plastic packaging and drop it on the floor – no matter where they're standing. Many parts of Asia, South America and Africa are overflowing with plastic waste because of this attitude towards littering. In India and Bangladesh, hundreds of cows die every year because they wander through the streets feeding on waste stored in plastic bags (and even a cow's strong stomach acid cannot digest polyethylene). While the mountains of rubbish grow in the developing world, the situation in Germany and many other European countries is completely different.

Germans are the recycling world champions. Anything that cannot be recycled goes into landfill. But everything else is separated and recycled. Organic waste (food scraps, teabags, coffee grounds etc.) is put in the brown or green bin (depending on where you live). Paper goes into a special paper bin, and glass and bottles go into a separate recycling container. Then, there is the 'Green Dot' waste. This is a German scheme that allows manufacturers to contribute towards the recycling costs of their packaging. A green recycling logo on the packaging lets the consumer know that the packaging is recyclable. Most 'Green Dot' recycling is made up of plastics. Each and every yoghurt pot and butter tub is carefully washed and thrown into the yellow sack of the yellow recycling bin. Some of this plastic may still end up as landfill, but the majority of it will end up at a recycling centre where it will be sorted. The different plastics are compacted into balls, and suddenly go through a remarkable transformation. No longer is the plastic mere waste, but a valuable commercial material that can sell for up to €400 euros (around £325 pounds) a tonne. The plastic waste, or rather, valuable raw material, is then loaded onto container ships and usually sent to Asia. In the warehouse of the oil refinery in Chittagong, for example, is a container filled with exactly this type of recycled plastic from Germany.

It's the afternoon after the morning's demonstration. The booking desk at the police headquarters in Chittagong is in the basement where it's dark and humid. Mohmin is locked in a small room with 20 other demonstrators. None of them know what's going to happen to them and they are all very scared. The seconds feel like minutes, and the minutes feel like hours. One after another they are taken away from the cell – and they don't return. *Is that a good or bad sign?* the men wonder. Finally, Mohmin is led into a dark room, empty of furniture except for a table and two chairs. Mohmin has to give the police his full name, his address, and tell them where he works. "Who put you up to this?" they ask him over and over again.

In the eyes of the police, the secret service and the government, it's not the terrible state of the country that's to blame for the demonstrations and the strikes, but some kind of evil ringleader who's turning the poor against the government. *Crack!* Mohmin's interrogator slaps him so hard his ears won't stop ringing. What's he supposed to say? Mohmin doesn't know of any strike ringleader. One of his colleagues, Abdul told him about the strike. But he's obviously not the ringleader . . . *Crack!*

While Mohmin is still in the dark interview room, Kholil has managed to sneak back into work. In the recycling yard are endless containers. They are filled to the brim with balls of squashed plastic waste from Europe. The workers move the balls to the shredder to be cut up. The shredder turns the plastic into tiny flakes. These flakes are then washed and placed onto a conveyer belt. Kholil and many other young people stand at the conveyer belt and sort the flakes by hand. The coloured flakes are thrown to the left to be turned into sheets of plastic and packing materials. The white flakes are thrown to the right to be turned into a colourless yarn that can be dyed later. Kholil is trying to work faster than everybody else today. He wants to show his bosses how much he wants to work there. He's too scared to go to a demonstration ever again, and he can't help wondering, *What's happened to Mohmin?*

25 August 2005

After a long interview, Mohmin is finally released. He manages to make it to work on time for the early shift, but he's anxious they won't let him in. His cheek is swollen and he has a black eye. The door opens, and standing next to one of the guards is the boss of the company. He approaches Mohmin.

"What's your name?" he demands.

"Mohmin."

"I'm assuming you didn't show up yesterday so you could go to the demonstration?"

Mohmin doesn't answer and averts his gaze.

"I should have you fired!" shouts his boss. "But I have no one to work the spray nozzle and we've got so many orders I need *everyone* to work extra shifts. The weavers need to produce a lot of fleece, and suddenly everyone wants our polyester yarn. So get to it!"

Mohmin rushes off and says a prayer of thanks.

"I'm keeping my eye on you!" his boss shouts after him.

Mohmin goes over to the oven where the polyethylene granules made from crude oil are combined with recycled plastic from Germany. He's in charge of running the machine and making sure everything in the oven is at the correct temperature. He opens the right nozzles to produce extremely thin polyester fibres. Mohmin guides the threads through a cooling fan where they harden, but keep their elasticity. The polyester fibres are finally wound onto spools. The polyester that will be turned into fleece receives one more treatment. The fibres are distressed, so that they become thick and fluffy. These synthetic fibres have a special significance for

Bangladesh. Seventy five per cent of the country's exports are textiles, even though Bangladesh can't produce cotton. Cotton has to be imported which shrinks the manufacturing companies' profits. Instead, the textile industry in Bangladesh started producing new products in the last decade, synthetic fibres, notably polyester. Forty per cent of the world's textiles are made from artificial fibres. As Bangladesh has its own crude oil source, it can produce synthetic fibres, such as the material for my fleece, without having to import expensive raw materials.

5

Tuk-tuk Races, Floods and Fleece: A Day in Bangladesh's Textile Industry

1 September 2005

Outside the Hotel Intercontinental in Dhaka, Bangladesh's capital city, about 30 taxi drivers are swarming upon three European factory owners as they leave the building. All the drivers are trying their luck, anxious to gain the custom of the foreigners, or the 'bideshi' as they call them. Instead, the Europeans ignore the crowd of drivers, and get into Hassan's taxi, as he's the only driver waiting patiently in his tuk-tuk.

There are thousands of these motorised, three-wheeled taxis in Asia, and everyone calls them tuk-tuks. The reason for this is clear as soon as the motor starts running. It makes a chugging sound that gets faster and faster and louder and louder, *tuk-tuk-tuk-tuk-tuk*, shaking the driver, passengers and luggage before they've even started moving. Once the journey starts, they race through the streets, squeezing down even the narrowest roads that cars can't go down. Although when the ground is flooded, they often get stuck in the mud. It can take two or three people to pull them free!

Tuk-tuks have a canopy overhead and can carry between two and six people. If necessary, they also carry large loads of rice, newspapers or furniture. If you're a lucky tuk-tuk driver, like Hassan, you might get to ferry some bideshi around. Foreigners are always willing to pay a lot more for fares than locals. Although whatever Hassan earns, most of it will have to be given away almost immediately. Like most tuk-tuk drivers, Hassan's taxi was bought with loaned money. The private loan company adds 10 per cent interest to what he still owes them, every month! This is why Hassan has to accept every job that comes his way. The Europeans want to go to a mill on the outskirts of the city. One of them asks him to drive, "Straight there, as quickly as possible!" The request for speed is completely unnecessary. Hassan's livelihood depends on the fact that he drives one of the fastest tuk-tuk's in Dhaka.

Tuk-tuks may only have three wheels, but they also have exceptionally loud horns. On the streets of Bangladesh, a vehicle's horn is almost as important as its engine: the louder the better. *Beep Beep!* goes Hassan's horn, telling pedestrians and other traffic to get out of the way, his tuk-tuk is coming through, and fast! A pleasant breeze takes the edge off the scorching heat, making the palm trees the tuk-tuk is driving past start to sway. The palm trees are growing in small gardens in front of rows of white painted houses. Are we still in Bangladesh? Yes. But Hassan's tuk-tuk is speeding through one of the most affluent parts of Dhaka, known as Dhanmondi.

Around 14 million people live in and around Dhaka. And at least half of them live in slums. Bangladesh is always portrayed the same way by the media, as a country suffering from floods, poor living conditions and hunger. But Bangladesh is also home to beaches, national parks, and mountains and forests where Bengal tigers can still be found. Not far from Dhanmondi, the view from the tuk-tuk is dramatically different: a sprawling slum with shoddily built factories lurking in the background like huge shadow puppets. Most of them are textile factories, as the region surrounding Dhaka specialises in textile production.

Hassan is taking his European passengers to visit one of these factories. In fact, the bideshi are heading to the very same factory where *our* polyester yarn is being treated. A whole lorry load of yarn was transported from Chittagong to Dhaka four days ago, to be turned into fleece material. Even though it's daytime and the factory is vast, it's dark and sticky inside the building. A rhythmic clicking and clacking sound fills the enormous production room, where a few workers move deftly between the mechanical looms. These vast machines work exactly like hand-operated looms: rows of threads are stretched lengthways and are alternately moved up and down so that a shuttle carrying a cross-thread can be pushed through. The woven threads are then combed to create small loops in the fabric, which are then trimmed, leaving multiple tiny, soft bristles. These bristles are then scoured in order to open up the fibres and make the fleece fluffy and soft. All the trapped air between the fibres works as an excellent insulator. When it's finished, the newly produced fleece material is rolled up into 40 kilogram bolts.

Forty-five minutes later, Hassan drops off his passengers at the factory. Usually he would charge the bideshi four or five times the standard fare, but unluckily for him, a guard at the factory takes care of all taxi payments and he knows exactly how much the fare should be. On the up side, Hassan receives a new fare straight away. But instead of people, he's transporting rolls of fleece. The cabin and the luggage rack are loaded up by four workers from the factory, and the tuk-tuk groans under the weight of it all. While Hassan and the guards watch the taxi being loaded up with bolts of fleece, the owner of the textile factory arrives in his brand new Mercedes

Benz. The guard closest to Hassan says, "Life's only easy for factory owners, politicians and generals. There are no good jobs for anyone else! Why does Allah let this happen?" Hassan just shrugs and gets into his tuk-tuk. He doesn't disagree with the guard exactly, but he does think that not all bad jobs are equally 'bad'. Being a guard, for example – he believes – is a fairly good job, for a 'bad' job. True, the pay isn't great, but all you have to do is stand around, drink tea, chat with people and tell off the workers if they're late or disruptive. The place he's about to drive to now is where the *really* 'bad' jobs are – the fabric dyeing factory. He gets into his tuk-tuk and gives it some gas.

The drive to the dyeing factory isn't a particularly nice journey. He passes slums and run-down factories that have suffered badly from the heavy monsoon rain. Whole floors of the factories are still flooded, and the road is littered with water-filled potholes. It's a very bumpy ride. When he arrives, the guards make sure Hassan doesn't get to see much of the factory or what goes on there. Really, you just have to take a look at the water coming out of the drains at the back of the factory to find out. Sometimes it's red, other days it's blue or green, whatever colour the factory is using under the cover of darkness. The local water supply is poisoned by the chemicals that this factory, and others, are dumping directly into rivers and drains. Just washing in the water here can make people sick. The only relatively safe drinking water comes from underground wells, but during the monsoon season, overspill from the rivers can contaminate the wells.

Despite the guards' secrecy, Hassan knows what really happens in the huge dyeing workshop. Someone from his town told him. Inside are lots of tanks the size of small swimming pools. They are filled with lime, toxic bleaches and a variety of dyes. First the fabric is bleached to make it really white, so that the dyed colour will be really bright. Usually, the fabric is transported into the tanks of dye by machine, but the workers – often children – frequently have to put their bare arms into the machines to sort out blockages. The workers then climb into the tanks of poisonous dyes and stamp on the fabric with their bare feet. After being dyed, the fabric is hung up to dry on washing lines that are hundreds of metres long.

Fleece material gets a final extra treatment. It's pulled through a tank filled with a solvent to make sure that bobbles don't form on the fibres later on.

15 September 2005: 7:45am

Hassan is back at the dyeing factory with his tuk-tuk. Five freshly-dyed rolls of fleece are loaded onto his taxi. One roll, which is smaller than all the others, is bright red. Once everything's been loaded up, Hassan drives his tuk-tuk through the factory gate and heads towards the Bangladesh Garni International (BGI) textile factory.

At the same time, outside the BGI textile factory, hundreds of seamstresses are waiting to start work. The doors will open in ten minutes. It's quite difficult for most of the seamstresses to make sure they arrive on time, as many don't have watches, and there are no clocks on the streets. Hassan reaches the factory just before half past eight. The gates open and he drives in. Just as the gate is closing again, a worker slips through. It is 17-year-old Taslima, who dashes into the factory and races up the stairs to her floor. One of the guards shouts after her: "You wretched toad! Next time I'll slam the door in your face!" That's what it's usually like here: the young seamstresses – all between 16 and 30 years old – are not treated kindly by the management.

Taslima works on the second floor where over 80 sewing machines stand in two long rows. She settles herself at her workstation right in the middle. This is where she will sit for the next eight to twelve hours doing nothing but sewing. There's already a stack of pre-cut fleece pieces piled behind her: for the last two days her department has been trying to fulfil a massive order for fleece body warmers. She takes the back section of a fleece and places the right hand front section, with a pocket already sewn into it, on top. *Tack,*

tack, tack, tack, she's already stitched the shoulder. She sews the pieces together down one side. *Tack, tack, tack, tack.* And now the same for the left hand side . . . Taslima's glad to be able to work at a sewing machine. For the first half of the year she was only a sewing assistant. This meant she had to help five seamstresses, but was only paid half of what they were. She learnt quickly however, and when a seamstress from her group left – suddenly she had a sewing machine of her own.

Tack, tack, tack, tack. Taslima sews the collar on, and then sews up the bottom of the fleece. The zip is the final piece to be sewn in. The first of the countless fleeces that she will make today is finished. No one has even told her off for being late! Sometimes, when a seamstress is late for work they dock her wages, but Taslima has been lucky today. The workshop is packed, badly lit and there's barely any fresh air. As the monsoon season has just come to an end, there's water everywhere. It smells of mould and it's unbearably hot. The mere effort of breathing makes you break into a sweat, and if you're working hard, the sweat runs in small rivers down your back. By the second or third fleece, Taslima's hands are working automatically. In her mind she flees this dark, sticky room and runs back to her family. They live outside in the countryside, a three-hour drive away by minibus. Every two or three months she gets a couple of days off so she can travel home to visit them. Often when she's there the whole community gather at her uncle's house to watch the only television in the village. In Bangladesh there are approximately six televisions for every hundred people, and in the countryside that statistic is even lower. Whole villages watch TV together – it's a social event. Bizarrely, up to three quarters of airtime is taken up by advertising. It's insane to think that so many adverts are shown in a country where over half the population live on less than €1.50 euros (around £1 pound) a day, and will never be able to afford new cars, mobile phones, posh mustard or designer cosmetics.

On the other hand, public television channel BTV shows lots of interesting programmes, including Taslima's favourite show, a cartoon series called *Meena*. *Meena* is loved by girls and young women across Bangladesh. The 10-year-old protagonist, Meena, is a brave and outgoing young woman. She likes going to school, is the smartest member of her family and fights the oppression of women in Bangladesh. She campaigns against young girls getting married, and raises awareness about issues such as the lack of education that women are given, or the fact that girls are rarely taken to a doctor when they're ill. Girls and women usually watch TV on their own. If any men are about, they usually complain about what the women are watching. They don't like programmes like *Meena*. They want their women to stay at home, obey their husbands, and if they *must* work, to hand over their wages with no questions asked.

Low Pay, High Risk
11/12 April 2005

In the middle of the night, a nine-storey textile manufacturing company collapses in Savar, a suburb of Dhaka. The building must have been poorly constructed, as it had only been completed a few months previously. The rescue teams who come to help don't have any proper rescue equipment. Instead they have to search for the trapped workers using just their hands. Tragically, this results in a death toll of 61, with over 100 workers seriously injured.

But why is the number of casualties so high? In Bangladesh, there are frequently no working emergency exits at factories. The majority of the 3,000 factories that produce goods for export, such as my fleece body warmer, do not meet legal safety requirements. Most factories only have one entrance and exit, which is closed during working hours so that no one can sneak in or out.

With crowded rooms, bad lighting, and poor safety procedures, is it any wonder that there are so many major accidents in the manufacturing industry? Over the last decade, official accident logs suggest that hundreds of textile workers have been killed and thousands have been badly injured, but the real figures could be even higher. And these numbers don't take into account minor injuries, for which there are no records.

Around two million people work in the textile industry, and 90 per cent of them are young women under the age of 25. They have to work up to 100 hours a week! In Europe, the average full-time working week is only 41.6 hours long. In Bangladesh in 2010, the national minimum wage was raised to 3000 taka (around €19.80 euros/£16.00 pounds) per month. Despite this, the majority of the average seamstresses' wages is still spent on rent. In order to support their families, textile workers must work overtime, and lots of it. However they are rarely fully compensated for the overtime they do, and sometimes they aren't paid for it at all. Often, the only bonus is that they get to keep their job. On top of working long hours, female workers are frequently harassed and sometimes even beaten by their supervisors. This is why they keep striking. They want better treatment in the workplace, and a higher minimum wage, one that they and their families can live on. At the same time, the factory owners are feeling the pressure of worldwide competition. They are determined to keep trying to achieve the impossible: to make better quality clothing for less and less money.

15 September 2005: 1:00pm

Tack, tack, tack, tack! Men have the final word at Taslima's factory too. The seamstresses aren't allowed to stand up without permission from a male supervisor. They're not allowed to go to the toilet without permission. They're not even allowed to talk! The seamstresses are constantly being harassed – and today the supervisors are particularly angry. But why? *Tack, tack, tack, tack.* After a million stitches – or that's what it feels like to Taslima – comes the long-awaited announcement of the lunch break. "Half an hour, and not a second longer!" cry the supervisors. The workers leave their desks and gather into small groups. Everyone eats and talks at the same time. A message is passed from group to group, "Everyone working on the fleece body warmer job has to have them finished by the end of the day. No one is allowed home until the order is complete!" *Oh no*, Taslima thinks to herself, throwing her leftover rice and vegetables onto to the floor in anger. Meanwhile, many women make use of their short lunch break to queue up for the toilet. They don't know when they'll get another chance to go.

Tack, tack, tack, tack . . . Taslima is back at her workstation. She'd barely started to recover from the morning's workload before she had to get back to work. Luckily she's still young, and has enough energy to carry on. Taslima is determined to make a success of this job: under no circumstances does she want to end up like her mother. Her mother has eight children and stays at home all day. After she's cooked, she lets everyone else eat first, then eats whatever is leftover. Which usually isn't much. Taslima and her sister are the first members of their family who can read and write. With help from their relatives, Taslima's parents could buy a small piece of land where they could build a hut and her mother could have a small vegetable garden. But instead, her parents choose to farm for a living. This means they have to rent farmland, for which the landlords demand half of the yearly harvest as payment. To survive during the monsoon season, Taslima's father goes to Dhaka or Chittagong to work as a labourer. It's a very hard life.

Taslima is determined to do things differently. One day, she plans to take out a small loan from the Grameen Bank.

This is a very unusual bank based in Bangladesh that provides low interest loans to local people. The lending criteria are simple. Firstly, they do not loan money to people who already own land, a business or a tuk-tuk. Secondly, they *only* loan money to women. The Grameen Bank believe that women are hit hardest by poverty, and are therefore more likely to be careful how they spend their money. The supervisor's voice interrupts Taslima's thoughts as it echoes from the other end of the room: "What? You want to go to the toilet again? I don't think so. You're just trying to get out of work!"

8:00pm

Even though the normal shift of 10 to 12 hours is over, no one on Taslima's floor is allowed to stop working. The order for 1,000 fleeces for a German company has to be finished by the end of the night so it can ship tomorrow. *Tack, tack, tack, tack* . . . Yet another collar seam finished! Taslima is exhausted, she can barely lift her arms, they're as heavy as two large jugs of water. Now and again her eyelids droop and close and she daydreams, although scary thoughts keep invading her mind . . . Thoughts of water coming flooding in from all sides, bursting through the doors and the walls while her and her family lie sleeping!

Every year, her parent's house is waterlogged by the

monsoon and half-destroyed by storms and hurricanes. Because it's always being rebuilt in a hurry, it's built out of easily sourced materials such as mud, straw, bamboo and plastic sheeting. Last year however, the monsoon was worse than usual. A lot worse. The flood lasted for an exceptionally long time – from the beginning of July until the middle of September. The rivers burst their banks and flooded first the low-lying land and then everywhere else. At the height of the flood, whole villages looked like small islands in a huge ocean. The streets were underwater, the factories were closed . . . It was only possible to travel if you had a boat. And it got worse: even though everyone was surrounded by water, there was hardly any clean drinking water available. It was difficult to cook meals, and all the women in the village had to share the one dry stove available.

In August the water didn't subside like it usually did, but began to rise further. Taslima's family quickly built a small, raised platform so that the family and their only cow had somewhere safe to sleep. They were woken one night by the water rushing into the house and the mud walls collapsing. Taslima and her siblings were left standing waist deep in water. In the morning, her family left the hut and went to live with relatives in town for weeks, until the flood subsided. During this period, the only way they could survive was by taking out a loan. This was a very expensive decision. The local money-lender adds 20 per cent in interest to their outstanding debt, every month! Even now, Taslima's parents are using some of Taslima's wages to help pay back the debt. *Tack, tack, tack . . .*

"OUCH!" Taslima is startled. She has hurt her hand with the sewing machine needle. When seamstresses are tired, accidents with needles and the sharp cutting knives happen far more frequently. "That must never, *never* happen again!" Taslima scolds herself. Since she's been working at the factory, her family have been better off than ever before. Taslima doesn't ever give leaving this job a second thought. Even when she is almost overcome with exhaustion, she wipes the tears from her eyes, thinks of her family, and keeps working.

11:05pm

Taslima and her colleagues have been sewing for 16 hours. Their only break was for half an hour at lunchtime. So far, only 889 body warmers are finished. Taslima has needed to go the toilet badly for hours, but the supervisor hasn't let anybody leave the room since 8:00pm. Instead he complains the whole time. "You're so pathetic, work faster!" he grumbles. The rolls of green, blue, grey and brown fleece are getting thinner. Taslima hopes there will be enough material left to get the job done. *Tack, tack, tack, tack . . .*

16 September 2005: 1:10am

The rolls of fleece have all been used up. There are only small scraps left at the cutting table. The foreman screams at the cutters, "You fools! You've cut the pieces too large! I'll be taking this out of your wages!" Taslima cannot bear it. She stands up and runs along factory aisles looking for usable fleece. What would *Meena*, her heroine, do now? Then Taslima spots the small roll of bright red fleece. "Over here! There's some left!" she cries. She drags the roll out of the corner.

"That's bright red!" the cutter protests.

"It doesn't matter! Surely Germans like red too!" says Taslima.

"Men in red fleeces? Really?" says one of the cutters, looking to the supervisor for instructions.

"I don't care!" spits the supervisor. "Just get it done so we can all go home . . ."

So they use the red fleece. *Tack, tack, tack, tack* . . . In a flash there are 11 bright red fleece body warmers. No sooner has *my* fleece come into the world it's packed into a cardboard box, ready to be shipped to Germany. It might have been a horrible day's work for the seamstresses, but none of them would give up their jobs for anything . . .

6

A World of Floating Metal Boxes: A Container Ship Heading for Europe

16 September 2005

For two weeks, a red metal container has been sitting in the yard of the textile factory on the outskirts of Dhaka. It is six metres long, 2.3 metres wide and 2.3 metres high. Day in and day out it has been loaded up with boxes of clothing fresh from the factory. It takes a long time to fill such a vast space. By the time it is full, there are thousands of items of clothing inside. Along with the body warmers, there are jackets, tracksuits and pyjamas, all made from fleece. The container has acquired a number of dents and a lot of rust during its lifetime. It has travelled non-stop around the world for the last eight years.

At about 10:00am, three final boxes of fleece body warmers complete the container's load. It takes eight workers to close and lock the container door. They don't call up Hassan to pick up the load this time: his tuk-tuk is far too small to carry *this* container. Instead, it is loaded onto the back of a filthy, well-travelled lorry. The lorry will travel down Bangladesh's muddy streets, trying not to slide off the road, until it reaches the harbour in Chittagong. There the driver will offload the container, and instead of being loaded straight onto a ship, nothing will happen to it for several days. The container will sit on the dock, patiently, while the monsoon batters it. All too often, the factory staff work themselves to death to meet the shipping deadlines, only for the clothing to sit in the harbour, unmoving, for days and days. Has the container been forgotten about? No, it has not. For one particular customs officer, the container is all he can think about. There's something wrong with the paperwork. A section about the contents of the container has not been filled in properly, which means it will not be signed off by the Ministry of Agriculture for shipping the next day.

21 September 2005

After five days of tense phone calls, the owner of the textile factory finally comes to the harbour in person. The customs officer leaves him waiting for over an hour before explaining he hasn't provided an important document from the Office of Foreign Affairs. The factory owner has never even *heard* of this particular document before. He asks the customs officer if he can step into his office so they can talk about the situation in more detail. A small brown envelope exchanges hands. The factory owner goes for a cup of tea, and by the time he comes back, all of his papers are miraculously now 'in order'. According to Transparency International, a global organisation who campaign against government corruption, Bangladesh is one of the most corrupt countries in the world.

The Shipping Container Revolution

In 1956, the shipping container revolution began. American entrepreneur Malcolm McLean came up with a bright idea; instead of loading individual boxes of goods onto ships and trains, multiple goods could be packed into standard sized containers. These boxes would be much easier to load and unload than multiple individual units, and so the shipping container was born. A standard container, known as a TEU (twenty foot equivalent unit), is the same wherever you are in the world: six metres (20 feet) in length, 2.3 metres high, and equally as wide. A single container can hold up to 30 cubic metres of goods. Nowadays, there are also an increasing number of FEU (forty foot equivalent unit) containers in use, which are about 12 metres long.

Over the past 50 or so years, shipping containers have taken over the freight world: more than half of all goods are now transported in TEU containers. There's an estimated 20 million of them, making around 300 million individual journeys a year. Without these containers globalisation wouldn't exist – or at least not to this extent anyway. Ninety-five per cent of world trade is done via ocean freight. Commodities such as oil and iron are transported in specialised tankers and cargo ships, and many other goods, from raw materials through to finished products, waste and scrap are also transported via containers. In the freight industry, no one does anything without a financial incentive. 'Baksheesh', is the magic word. It is understood across the whole of Asia and Africa, and is the financial grease that gets you out of *tight* situations.

22 September 2005

Six days after its arrival, the container is finally lifted by crane and moved down to the dock, where the container ship *Dhaka* had dropped anchor. The *Dhaka*, which can carry up to

250 containers, is called a 'feeder ship'. Feeder ships are the postmen of the container freight world: small and able to travel through shallow water. As the *Dhaka* only has a depth of 4.5 metres, she can pass through the majority of the shallow rivers on the Asiatic coast. Even at low tide, she can leave the harbour in Chittagong and head down the Karnaphuli River to the Bay of Bengal.

The *Dhaka* heads south and always stays close to land. Looking out from the ship's bridge, you can see a long white ribbon along the coast: Cox's Bazar. This sandy beach is 125 kilometres long, making it the longest unbroken sandy beach in the world. But there are rarely any tourists enjoying it. Holidaying in Bangladesh? No way. When Westerners hear the word Bangladesh, all they think of is floods and people starving.

25 September 2005

Three uneventful days pass by. The weather has been good, there have been no incidents on board the ship, and the coast still stretches out across the horizon. Somewhere in the distance behind the *Dhaka* is the border between Burma and Thailand. Despite the hassle-free journey, the mood on the ship is tense. The closer the *Dhaka* gets to the Strait of Malacca, the more ill at ease the captain and his crew become. This isn't an easy route to travel through, especially for small and medium freighter ships like the *Dhaka*. The Strait of Malacca is pirate territory.

All ships wanting to make their way from the West (Europe, Africa, the Far East, India) to the East (China, the Philippines and Japan) have to travel through this narrow stretch of water to reach the South China Sea. Hemmed in by Malaysia and Indonesia, the Strait of Malacca is almost 1,000 kilometres long and at points, only 25 kilometres wide. Approximately 50,000 ships travel through this narrow strait every year, and half of *all* pirate attacks happen here. Most people imagine pirates as being consigned to history. But that's not true. Instead of using sailing ships and flying Jolly Roger flags, they prefer inconspicuous fishing boats or small speedboats. Their attacks are fast and brutal. Everyone on board the *Dhaka* is sweating with anxiety, especially the captain. He has been attacked by pirates once before. The scar on his left hand is a constant reminder of that horrible day. He was badly beaten, and forced to open the ship's vault by men armed with guns and machetes. Every small boat that sails past makes his heart beat faster.

After 10 hours or so, the tense atmosphere finally lifts. It is the middle of the night when a glittering theatre of light suddenly appears in front of the *Dhaka*. Where, moments before there was only darkness, suddenly there are hundreds of columns of light. The sound of helicopters and car horns carry across to the ship on the breeze. There is the scent of rain after it has evaporated from warm streets. This is unmistakably Singapore, the small city-state at the most southern point of the Asiatic mainland.

Singapore was built as a centre for world trade by the British over 250 years ago, and today, Singapore has the largest container harbour in the world. This is where the axes of world trade cross paths: from the Far East to Europe, from the Far East to Southeast Asia/the East, and from the Far East to Australia. Around 20 million containers pass through this port each year, and that number increases annually. That's about 63,000 containers *every* day. A harbour is only capable of moving this much cargo by being exceptionally well organised. Singapore itself is renowned for being a very orderly and well-run city. For example, it is illegal to drop used chewing gum on the streets, and smokers may only partake in their favourite habit in specially designated glass booths. Everything runs like clockwork here. Within five hours the *Dhaka* has been unloaded.

27 September 2005

The container from Bangladesh holding the fleece body warmers only has to wait 21 hours before a crane loads it into the depths of a huge freighter. The *World Star* has dropped anchor in the dock. It's one of the world's newest and most state of the art container ships: at 312 metres long, it can hold up to 8,400 containers. The *Dhaka* was only delivering to a single destination – which in shipping terms is a fairly straightforward process. It's a completely different matter when you have 8,400 containers to deliver to 12 different destinations. Not only must the containers be unloaded correctly at all 12 harbours, but new containers must be loaded on in their place.

Loading the ship to result in as few container moves as possible during loading and unloading is a real art form. This is organised at the shipping company's headquarters by engineer Walter Smith. Although Walter is an expert in calculating optimum loading arrangements, the process can still take several days. Once the final loading plan is agreed, boarding engineer Philipp Connor monitors the loading and unloading of each container on his computer screen. On screen, the containers are colour coded by destination: red containers go to Jeddah (Saudi Arabia), green to Barcelona (Spain), yellow to Southampton (England), violet to Rotterdam (the Netherlands), and blue to Hamburg (Germany – where our fleece container is going). Empty containers are coloured grey, but are usually only found on the journey from Europe to Asia. Containers loaded with dangerous substances are highlighted as hazardous, and stowed in a particularly safe area of the ship.

During loading and unloading, the boarding engineer has to keep a close eye on the distribution of weight across the ship. The ship cannot be allowed to list (sit lower in the water on one side than the other). If too many containers are loaded on either the port or starboard side, he must stabilise the ship by filling the ballast tank on the opposite side with water. About 2,000 containers need to be loaded and unloaded in Singapore. The *World Star* has exactly 20 hours to complete this process. Twenty hours – that's 1,200 minutes, which works out at just over 30 seconds to move *each* container. When the *World Star* leaves Singapore, it is carrying 8,023 containers, arranged in 19 rows. Each row is composed of up to 25 blocks. In these blocks, containers are piled on top of one another from the bottom of the ship up to the 15th or 17th decks. A single block can be up to 40 metres high – as tall as a nine-storey house. Our fleece container is tucked in the middle of the ship: row 15, block 12, fourth storey.

Container Ships

In 2007, there were 3,500 container ships spread across the globe. Yet by 2017, it is predicted that a further 5,000 container ships will have been built and put into use. In 2005, the largest freighters could carry 8,400 TEU containers. By 2006, the *Emma Mærsk*, at 387 metres in length, could carry up to 15,200 TEU containers. And in 2011, the same company ordered 10 container ships with a capacity of 18,000 containers to be built.

Until the 1970s, Europe led the way in shipbuilding. But Japan soon took the lead – producing ships both faster and more cost-effectively. By the 1990s, Korea had overtaken Japan. The majority of orders for tankers and container ships went to Korea. These days, it looks like China will soon take the shipbuilding title from the Koreans. European shipbuilding, for example in Germany, is generally more specialised, focusing on feeder ships (smaller cargo ships) and passenger ferries.

28 September 2005

Half an hour behind schedule, the *World Star* leaves the harbour terminal in Singapore and enters the Strait of Malacca. It is night, and the crew are on high alert. However, they aren't as afraid as the crew of the *Dhaka* were. Large freighters like the *World Star* are much more difficult for pirate crews to attack, as they are as tall as tower blocks and fly through the narrow strait at 24 or 25 knots (about 45 kilometres per hour). Despite its speed and massive scale, the *World Star* does have one weak spot: the quarterdeck. This open deck at the back of the ship is situated closer to the water than the ship's side-walls. It's used to take on supplies at port, but it can also be used by pirates to gain access to the ship.

When a small, unknown ship approaches the rear of the *World Star*, Captain Neubold sounds the pirate alarm. Eight members of the crew run to the quarterdeck and release the huge water hoses that are used to fight fires on board. If intruders try to get on board, the crew will shoot them with powerful water jets from the hoses into the sea. Perhaps the pirates suspected the crew were prepared for them, or perhaps they were only harmless fishermen racing the freighter for fun? Either way, the *World Star* is spared.

Every month, five or six pirate attacks are reported in Southeast Asia. If pirates succeed in boarding and taking a 200 to 300 metre ship, they can make a lot of money. Sometimes they tie up the crew and rob the safe. More often than not they kidnap the crew and demand a ransom. Sometimes, they give the ship a different name and unload it at a port where paperwork isn't high on the customs officers' list of priorities. A list of ships that have recently gone missing, known as 'phantom' ships, is pinned up in the control room of the *World Star* as a constant reminder of the threat of pirates.

30 September 2005

Eight hours ago, the *World Star* finally left the Strait of Malacca, and has set a course of west-south-west. The risk of pirate attacks has passed, but now the crew are faced with a new threat: boredom. All they have to do is stay on a direct course for 3,000 kilometres, across the middle of the Indian Ocean. Then they will change course, and head for the Red Sea.

This is a good time to learn more about the *World Star*. The *World Star* is owned by a German shipping business, but sails on behalf of a group of Norwegian companies. The group of Norwegian companies are run by an Austrian boss, who is based at their headquarters in Hong Kong. The ship flies the flag of Panama, the captain is German, the on-board engineer is British and the rest of the crew are from the Philippines. The ship was built at the Daewoo shipyard in South Korea, and is currently carrying goods from China, India, Thailand and Bangladesh. It is also carrying Australian goods to be shipped to markets in Saudi Arabia, Egypt, Spain, the United Kingdom, the Netherlands, Germany and the Baltic region.

Logistics in the Age of Globalisation

Our fleeces and their raw materials will have travelled over 25,000 kilometres before reaching their final market destination of Hamburg. That is a relatively short journey compared to many other products. The individual materials that make up a thermos flask, for example, may travel up to three times around the *world* before the finished flask reaches its marketplace.

Experts at large companies are constantly asking: how can we break down the production process to make it more cost effective? Where are the cheapest raw materials and manufacturers? Where is the best value workforce? The success or failure of globalised production is all down to the cost of transporting materials around the world. Thanks to container ships, transport costs are so low they have virtually no impact on profits.

How much does it cost to transport a bottle of wine from Australia to Europe? In 2005, it cost €1,000 euros (about £675 pounds) to send a shipping container from Asia to Europe. Nine hundred and ninety-nine crates of wine, each holding six bottles of wine, can fit into a single shipping container. This works out at a shipping cost of €0.16 euros (about £0.10 pounds) per bottle. To send a fleece body warmer from Asia to Europe costs even less, only five or ten euro cents per item. The difference in cost depends on how well the container is packed. If oil does start running out in the next few years, the price of shipping will rise. No one really knows how much longer the individual materials that make up a thermos flask can be sent three times around the world before entering the marketplace.

5 October 2005

The *World Star* has left Saudi Arabia's container port in Jeddah two hours late. Although the ship can carry up to 8,400 containers, and left Singapore with 8,023 containers, the number has now dropped to 7,923. One hundred containers have been 'extinguished' (removed and not replaced) in Jeddah. If these containters were placed in one long line, they'd cover a distance of 48 kilometres – about the same distance as from Düsseldorf to Cologne (or central London to Gatwick Airport).

Though container ships filled with yellow, blue and red metal boxes seem boring on the outside, the contents of the containers themselves are fascinating. From Australian wines to electrical appliances to tonnes of fabric, the containers can hold absolutely anything. Removal companies are also using shipping containers more and more frequently, for customers who spend their lives having to travel for work from Europe to Asia or vice versa.

The crew can only guess at what goods the *World Star* is carrying based on the cargo list. From the outside, all 7,923 containers are identical. But what's going on with container C 53-786-23-894 in the fourth row, fifth level up? A red fluid is leaking out of it and running down the other containers in its block. It looks like it's bleeding. According to the cargo list, the container is filled with animal furs heading to Spain. It appears the furs have been sent straight from the slaughterhouse without any further processing or preparation. The smell coming from the container is disgusting: they're really starting to stink.

While the cargo waits quietly, packed into colourful containers, the crew live in the high, white deckhouse at the ship's stern. Right at the top of Deck A (the top deck) is the bridge and the control room – the brain of the ship. Deck B is the ship's stomach, where the galley and the canteen are located. Deck C is reserved for communal spaces, such as a TV room and a gym. Decks D through to G are the private rooms of the captain and crew. Below them are the engine rooms, generators that produce the electricity to run the ship, and the ship's motor, which is as tall as a six-storey house. It provides 93,000 horsepower – that's the same amount of horse power as produced by 700 people carriers.

This powerful motor allows the ship to run exactly according to schedule. The docking space at each port needs to be booked and paid for in advance, so the *World Star* must hit specific times and dates. The crew can use the powerful engine to make up lost time at sea, flying across the water at 26 knots (48 kilometres) per hour.

Punctuality is especially important for the next leg of the journey: sailing through the Suez Canal. One hundred and fifty years ago, the canal was dug through the desert that separated the Mediterranean and the Red Seas. It is 195 kilometres long with an average width of 205 metres. These days, large container ships and tankers are so wide that the canal can only be sailed through in one direction at a time. The ships sail in convoy. If a ship misses its spot, it will have to wait for at least two days while ships from the opposite end of the canal make their way through. The *World Star* has managed to avoid this fate. It has made it across the Red Sea in good time to join the correct convoy.

10 October 2005

The *World Star* reaches the Spanish port of Algeciras, near Gibraltar. Five hours have been allocated to unload 300 containers. Only ten containers will be loaded back onto the ship. Even if more time was available, none of the crew would disembark here. The captain and his officers have to be there for the loading and unloading of the ship. It would be too expensive to hire a team to work overnight in Spain.

If the rest of the crew did decide to grab a taxi and have a few beers in a local bar, it would burn a big hole in their pockets. The majority of the crew aren't particularly well paid, and their families back at home receive the majority of their monthly wages of €1,000 to €1,200 euros (about £675 to £810 pounds). It's worth noting that although the ship's crew travel the world for a living, they don't actually get to see much of it. All ports look exactly the same. One of the few upsides of the job is that the shipping company pays for them to fly home to see their families every six months. Twice a year they see their wives, children and parents. The captain and the officers get an even better deal; they get to go home every three months.

12 October 2005

After the *World Star* has sailed through the Strait of Gibraltar and along the Iberian Peninsula; it crosses the Bay of Biscay and heads towards the English Channel. Suddenly, bad news comes from the galley. Chef Juan has discovered that they only have two meals worth of cabbage left! Cabbage with bacon and pork sausages is the crew's favourite meal. The captain considers good food and shared meals to be of the utmost importance in order to keep up morale on board and create a positive team atmosphere. After all, the 22 people on board have to work together to keep this steel giant of a ship under control. The journey has been smooth so far, but it has just been announced by the captain that the ship is heading into a severe storm.

In the Bay of Biscay, the heavy autumn storm takes hold. Now the captain has to decide whether the ship should change course or seek shelter in a port. He has been instructed to stay on course during storms of up to gale force 11. In light of this, he holds steady and the steel behemoth heads straight into a fog as thick as pea soup. As the *World Star* ploughs on through the rough seas, the containers awake as if from a long slumber. A chorus of screeching metal sings out across the ship as the containers sway and roll. Unfortunately, not all of the containers are singing the same tune. Container D 42-523-46-743 doesn't seem to like the singing of its neighbour M 53-987-12-853. It moves further and further away with each roll of the ship. The storm also increases the risk that the cold storage containers will lose their connection to the ship's power supply, causing their contents to defrost and be ruined. Every half an hour, the crew patrol the ship to make sure the containers aren't moving around too much. Finally, after seven long hours, the storm blows itself out and the weather becomes calm. The *World Star* is undamaged and still sailing according to schedule.

Was there ever any real danger to the ship or crew? Yes, there was. Every storm is dangerous. On average, two cargo ships sink *every week* due to poor weather conditions. Sometimes monster waves, 20 metres high, engulf them, dragging them under. The *World Star* passes the English Channel and reaches the North Sea. The captain stands outside and sniffs the air. Yes, it smells like home to him, nowhere else on the ocean is there so much iodine in the air. After crossing the North Sea, they will once again have to pass through a narrow stretch of water. They have to make their way up the River Elbe and hope that there are no traffic jams.

15 October 2005

Slowly but surely, the *World Star* makes its way up the Elbe. Ships the size of the *World Star* can only sail the 117 kilometres up the Elbe to the port of Hamburg when the North Sea tide is flowing upriver. The river is too shallow otherwise, and the *World Star* could easily run aground. Then comes a message the captain had been hoping not to hear: that their pre-booked docking place is occupied. How long will the *World Star* have to wait before it can dock? Two hours? Five hours? Delays like this are happening more and more frequently. The *World Star*'s shipping company, and many of the captain's colleagues, blame the ports for working too slowly.

But the captain knows the truth. The whole system is to blame. Last year, when the *World Star* started sailing, it was one of the largest container ships in existence, carrying up to 8,400 containers. In reality, the *World Star* is too big for a port like Hamburg, with its narrow shipping lanes and shallow water. But it's still expected to dock there. Now, shipping companies are building even larger ships that can carry up to 18,000 containers. The shipping companies believe that with larger ships, they'll make even more money, as they'll be able to reduce freight charges and beat the competition. They'll also, of course, be able to transport more cargo on every journey.

Where will it end? the captain wonders, as he gazes across the river to where a flock of cranes fly away.

7

From Surplus to Talisman: Something Unwanted Becomes a Lucky Charm

18 October 2005

Our off-white container is lifted out of the belly of the *World Star* by a huge crane, swung over a row of patiently waiting containers, and finally deposited on dry land. After a 12 hour wait in the third largest port in Europe, our cargo from Bangladesh is loaded onto a truck. Before leaving the port, the truck has to pass through customs. Information about the cargo had already been sent on ahead over the Internet, arriving long before the *World Star* docked at the quayside. The paperwork should list the exact contents of the container.

The customs officials check whether the data supplied is correct, but don't always do a thorough inspection of the contents of every container, otherwise all world trade would be infinitely delayed. Instead, they use their experience to decide which containers warrant further inspection. The officials use a large, powerful x-ray machine to scan the whole of a container, so they don't have to open each one up and crawl around inside. The x-ray produces an image on a computer screen, showing the outline of individual objects in different colours, depending on the type of material they are made from. Using this tool, the customs officials can work out exactly what is inside the container, and spot smuggled goods, illegal drugs, and sometimes even people that shouldn't be there!

It is the job of customs officials to make sure that import restrictions are observed. For example, when the World Trade Organisation's 'Agreement on Textiles and Clothing' ended in 2004, China flooded the European market with t-shirts, socks and jumpers. In response, the European Union implemented a strict limit on the quantity of these goods that could be imported from China. This needs to be monitored closely. Furthermore, there is the problem of fake goods. Initially, China was known for producing cheap products, but nowadays these are mostly counterfeit branded goods. Adidas trainers, for example, are copied down to the tiniest detail, which exasperates the official Adidas brand no end. As a result, customs authorities in Europe and America destroy all fake imports they come across.

Everyone for Themselves

The World Trade Organisation's 'Agreement on Textiles and Clothing' was created by the wealthiest industrialised nations in 1974. In order to protect their domestic textile companies from too much foreign competition, fixed limits were set on the imports of clothing from poorer, less industrialised nations, such as Eastern Europe, India and China. (The poorest countries in the world, like Bangladesh, were excluded from this limitation.) The countries affected by the import limits fought against this agreement, and the industrialised nations, whose vehicles and expensive consumer goods are all produced in Asia, eventually gave in, in 1995.

The 'Agreement on Textiles and Clothing' expired in 2004, and China promptly flooded the European and American markets with t-shirts, trousers, trainers and other similar items. At the same time, the export of clothing from Bangladesh fell by 25 per cent.

The customs officials don't find anything out of the ordinary in our container, so they let the truck drive through directly onto the A7 motorway, and then the A1. *Good*, the driver thinks to himself, pleased he won't have to drive through Hamburg during the morning rush hour . . .

19 October 2005

The department store distribution warehouse is near Gütersloh, Germany. The truck carrying our fleece body warmers delivered the container to a loading bay at the warehouse last night. Since 8:00am this morning, two assistants have been unloading it. For seven whole hours, the two men move back and forth, piling the boxes of clothing onto wooden pallets. Someone from the purchasing department emerges every now and then with a long list. He opens boxes and counts products, ticks things off on his list and disappears again. The clothing is unpacked and tagged in the warehouse storeroom. The body warmers are given the extremely reasonable price of €9.95 euros (about £6.70 pounds) and loaded onto a cart.

Erna and Brigitte work in the warehouse, sorting out the clothing from Bangladesh to be sent to the different stores across Germany. Whilst working, they talk about the most unpleasant of subjects: money – or more specifically, their lack of it.

"How am I supposed to get by on this?" Brigitte asks her colleague. "I earn six euros an hour – that means that, after tax, I don't even have €1,000 euros a month left in my pocket. Then there's income tax, health insurance and my pension. That leaves me with about €750 euros. If you add the rent, electricity and gas bills on top of that, I'm lucky if I have €350 euros a month to live on!"

"I hear you," Erna joins in. "I've worked here for fifteen years, and I still only get €1,500 euros a month. I have to feed three people with that. But if it makes you feel any better, I know people who earn even less than us. My friend Fabienne is a trained hairdresser, but she only makes about €680 euros a month at her salon, can you imagine? If customers didn't tip her, well, I don't even want to think about it . . ."

While they've been talking all the clothing has been allocated to specific stores, all except for the red fleece body warmers.

"Hey Erna, who ordered red fleeces?" Brigitte asks her co-worker.

"Red fleeces for men? That's an interesting purchasing decision?" says Erna.

They laugh.

"Should we call it in to head office?" wonders Brigitte.

"Nah, I have a better idea," says Erna. "We'll send one to Darmstadt, one to Dortmund – and the rest to the Hannover-Südstadt store – sorted!"

24 October 2005

In the department store in Hannover-Südstadt, the fleeces are selling well. The products were delivered just the day before by the firm's own truck. A saleswoman hung the fleeces on a special-offer rail right at the front of the store. The first fleece sold less than half an hour after opening. The brown body warmers, in sizes medium and large were the first to sell out, followed by the green ones. Finally, the last size medium blue fleece was sold too.

That same evening, I entered the store to buy something warm and cheap to wear in my office. I'm often asked, "What do you do for a living?" I say "I'm a journalist and a writer," which may sound impressive at first, until you realise that being a freelance writer does *not* pay well. It therefore comes as no surprise that I was immediately drawn to the cheap fleeces. But they didn't have any left in my size. Other bargain hunters had beaten me to it. Though when I realised that the red body warmers were also available in men's size medium, I still didn't buy one. I wouldn't be seen dead in a red fleece. Even on my second visit, still desperate for something warm to wear, I couldn't bring myself to buy a red one.

14 November 2005

After a two-week sale in the department store, there are only a few fleece body warmers left in stock. Size extra large in blue and green, and bright red fleeces in both medium and large.

The store manager assesses his stock. The winter jackets have been a real hit – there are only a few of them left. The fleeces have done well too, but the last few just aren't selling. He tells his staff, "Drop the price of these fleeces – let's say €8.00 euros."

I saw the special offer the very same day, and secretly planned to buy one the following morning.

12 January 2006

After breakfast I slip on my fleece body warmer and go into my office. The book that I completed at the end of the previous year is not quite finished: I have to take in some corrections that the publisher has asked me to make. While I edit the text, I think about how pleased I am with this fleece! I don't care how it looks, I don't have a mirror in my office. I'm so much warmer now. It's only when I go to the bathroom or fetch a book from the shelf in the living room that my girlfriend reminds me of how silly I look. Oh well, it's just a question of time. She'll be used to it in two or three weeks.

24 June 2006

This summer, the world's eyes are turned to Germany. It's the football World Cup and we are the host country. Football fans from Africa and South America are amazed at how clean everything is and how punctual the trains and buses are. Everyone celebrates together in homes, stadiums and bars, and even the footballers play fair, well . . . for the most part. The World Cup is a challenging time for me. I'm in the middle of writing a new book, which is what I should be concentrating on, but I also want to be part of Germany's ongoing World Cup party!

My red body warmer is resting on the back of my office chair. I'm wearing a different lucky charm for the World Cup: my yellow and black Dortmund football jersey that I was given as a present when I was a teenager. Today Germany are playing Sweden, and there's a small black and white television set up next to my computer screen. Unfortunately, on a black and white TV, it's very hard to distinguish the ball from the background. I sit in front of the computer and the mini-TV, trying to keep both screens in sight. Then it happens . . . Germany are making a break for the Swedish goal. I can't tell if it's Schweinsteiger or Klose who has the ball . . . the attacker shoots! I think the ball's gone in – I leap into the air, cheering in celebration, and my arm hits a bottle of red wine I'd left on a shelf behind me the night before. The wine spills, some of it lands on my fleece – and Germany haven't even scored a goal! So, this is how the stain ended up on my fleece. I couldn't wash it out, so I relegated the fleece to life inside my wardrobe, and promptly forgot all about it.

28 September 2006

My work's been going much more slowly than anticipated for the last few weeks. I get distracted far too easily. Why can't I concentrate? And since when have I been like this? I can't answer the first question, but I can give a precise answer to the second: since the day I put my red fleece in the wardrobe. I'm not a superstitious person, but I get my fleece out anyway, it's got to be worth a try, right? Writing seems so much easier all of a sudden. By the end of the day, I've written half a chapter. On top of this, I've also come up with a new idea for a book about globalisation. I know that my fleece is not really bringing me good luck. But the problem is, I have a *very active* imagination.

15 April 2007

Ta da! On my computer screen is a message of acceptance from my publisher. They want my globalisation book. I take out a piece of paper and brainstorm some initial thoughts. What does globalisation mean in practice? What do we think of when we think about globalisation? Moving jobs and work to where they can be done more cheaply. First to Eastern Europe, then to the Far East. This doesn't result in better pay for workers and more equal sharing of profits, but rather in increased damage to both people and the environment. Along with these negatives however, there are also positives. It means that new jobs are being created for people in underdeveloped regions of the world. Consumers in the developed West also benefit from globalisation, as many products have become much cheaper due to international manufacturing. Ideas, money, goods and people travel around the world . . . It's hard to say what *is* worthwhile and what *isn't*.

16 May 2007

Every working day begins with the same ritual. I prepare breakfast and open the manuscript I'd been working on the day before. Then I put on my fleece. Most of the time, I come up with a great idea while I eat breakfast. The research for the globalisation book is going well. Germany may not have become World Cup champions last year, but I have discovered that, in terms of machine production and many other industrial processes, Germany are unbeatable. Where do all the buttons for all the clothes made in China and Bangladesh come from? For the most part they're made in Bielefeld, Germany. The German Button Union is the world leader in this sector. Economics professor Hermann Simon calls companies such as this 'Hidden Champions'. They are hidden for two reasons: firstly, they are of no international interest as they only have around a hundred employees, and secondly, because they don't ever appear in the media.

'Hidden Champions' usually excel in areas that no one else is interested in. Who builds the most cigarette dispensers in the world? Korber Ltd. in Hamburg. Who builds 80 per cent of bridge cranes, like the ones used in the Hamburg container port? Kirow, a firm based in Leipzig. Who ships out the most shopping trolleys? Wanzl based in Leipheim. Who produces the largest wind turbines in the world, and in the greatest numbers? Enercoon in Aurich. Economic scientists have, up until now, found 1,316 examples of such 'Hidden Champions' – and they're finding more every day.

Winners or Losers of Globalisation?

Germany is simultaneously a winner *and* loser of globalisation. Over the last 25 years, Germany's unemployment levels have increased as more and more jobs have been outsourced abroad. These are predominantly in the coal and steel industries, but also in manufacturing and assembly plants. Assembly plants are factories where electrical equipment is put together, or clothes are sewn. Employers in Germany have taken the threat of overseas competition very seriously. To save money, employees are made redundant, and wages are either frozen or reduced. More recently however, fewer jobs have been outsourced to countries outside of Germany, and Germany is once again an attractive place for businesses to set up and grow.

Germany, as a nation, is rich. The country is worth approximately €5.4 billion euros! That would be €81,000 euros per person – if the money was distributed equally. In reality, 10 per cent of the population own 60 per cent of the nation's wealth, 40 per cent of the population own the other 40 per cent of the nation's wealth, and the other 50 per cent of the population have nothing or are in debt. Those who have money can capitalise on globalisation:

they can buy shares in businesses or set up new businesses. Those who have nothing on the other hand have to struggle to make ends meet. Globalisation is responsible for creating an ever-increasing gap between the rich and the poor. Most of the winners and losers can be separated into two kinds of people: the employees who have to work harder and harder, but don't receive any increase in payment for their efforts, and investors who profit from globalisation.

23 July 2007

It's been too warm to wear the fleece since June, so these days it just hangs on the back of my chair while I sit in my office researching my book about globalisation. Globalisation doesn't have a face; it's a creeping, ever-changing process that's hard to pin down and define. But this summer all that will change: the G8 Summit is taking place in Heiligendamm, Germany, near the Baltic Sea. The heads of state of the eight most important countries in the world are meeting to align their political and economic interests. These are the countries that drive globalisation above all others.

According to the World Trade Organisation (WTO), these heads of state speak with 'forked tongues'. By this, they mean that they say one thing, but do another. The WTO was formed by the United Nations as a neutral referee to keep an eye on globalisation. They know all too well that these industrialised nations will do everything they can to break down the trade barriers of poorer countries, while working just as hard to protect their own countries' production interests. The US for example, protects and subsidises its own domestic production, especially the cotton industry. This is so they can offer their cotton at a much lower price than farmers in Africa or Asia on the world market. At the same time, the US imposes an import tax on three quarters of all goods entering the country. In the same way, the European Union also subsidises many of its producers, such as the agriculture and fishing industries, in order to maintain its domestic industry.

2 September 2007

My quirky obsession with always having my fleece to hand has had some inevitable consequences: it looks battered and worn out and it's covered in marks and stains. I don't mind – but my girlfriend cant stand it! Instead of a greeting, whenever she comes home from work, I hear, "I've told you a thousand times, I don't want to come home and see you in that grubby body warmer! It's disgusting!"

"Why?" I always ask.

"Because even the stains have stains!" she cries.

"The stains aren't hurting anyone," I feebly protest. Although even I am aware that it looks pretty horrible.

"Well buy a new one!" she goes on. "It's not like it was expensive . . ."

It's true. Increasingly, we replace old things at the drop of a hat. What do you do when one of your household appliances breaks? Have it repaired? Why? It'll probably cost just about as much money to buy a new one. Mobile phones and computers become out of date within two years. And what about clothing that's stained, torn or has got too small? No one sews these days, so if something's damaged, no one will fix it. Plus it looks pretty uncool to wear something that's clearly been repaired. Thanks to globalisation, clothing is so cheap you can just buy something new, and throw away the old and broken stuff. But unlike most people, I won't be parted from my lucky charm, my grubby, red fleece body warmer.

6 November 2007

I come home one evening from a day trip, sit at my computer, feel around behind me for my fleece – and can't find it! It's not there. Maybe I left it in the kitchen. No!

Or in the living room? No. It's not in the bathroom either. I start to panic.

"Darling, have you seen my fleece?" I ask my girlfriend.

"Yeah, I washed it," she says, "but the stains really wouldn't come out this time, so I dropped it off at the clothing recycling bin on my way to –"

"My fleece!" I cry, interrupting her.

"Yes, I thought we agreed you were going to buy a new one!"

We agreed? I think, incredulously. *No, she had suggested that. Not me.*

"I wanted to keep at least a little bit of it for luck," I tell her, aware of how silly I sound.

"But no one would be able to wear it if it had a hole in it," she replies.

I don't have time to argue with her. "Did you put it in the container in Moltkeplatz?" I demand.

"Why? You're not actually going to go down there are you . . ."

I was already on my way out of the door. I cycled at top speed to the recycling container. It's a huge grey box with a charity logo on the front. Maybe I'll be able to get our bag of clothes back out of it. But when I get there, there's a truck parked beside it. Three men are sorting through the bags of clothes, but they don't look like charity workers to me. Then I remembered reading an article about how some charities no longer pick up the clothing from recycling bins themselves. They rent out the containers to firms who specialise in selling used clothing. I ask the men which company they work for. One of them gets annoyed with me and shouts, "It's none of your business!"

I walk back to my bike, but stay within watching distance. I'm not put off that easily. A lot of people give their old clothing to charity because they think it goes to a good cause. But does it really? The charity whose logo is on the front of this particular container has probably only licensed the clothing collectors to use their name and branding. It's likely they have nothing to do with the clothing once it's collected. So who's behind this business of selling our used clothes? I want to know, and I think about following them. But that would be pretty hard on a bike. I cycle home and look up the closest clothing recycling company in the *Gelben Seiten* – the Yellow Pages. All I need to do now is find them.

My investigation takes me to an industrial area on the

outskirts of the city. Behind a barred gate I can see a large yard filled with trucks and shipping containers. I get off my bike, call over one of the workers and ask to see the boss. Heiner Schulz comes over to me and asks what or who I'm looking for. I tell him that I'm looking for my fleece. "I'm sorry, but I can't let you in," he tells me. I decide to try another tack. I pull out my press pass and explain that I want to write a story about clothing recycling. It turns out that Heiner Schulz is a really nice guy. He speaks very openly about his company and the whole industry. We walk through the yard into a huge factory hall. It's filled with clothing, bed covers and balls of material. There's no sign of the charity's branding here.

"At first I thought you were looking for a job!" he laughs. "We don't have enough people at the moment, and two containers for Africa and one for Belarus are due."

"Well," I reply, "if the newspaper don't like my story, I might have to take you up on that offer!"

Schulz's recycled clothing business is very professional, and runs like clockwork. The old clothing is unloaded, unpacked and then sorted in the main hall. Over forty people are busy working. In front of them is a huge mountain of unsorted clothes. From morning until night they hold up one item of clothing after another, inspecting them, and then throwing them in one of up to 10 containers. There are three standards of quality: things that are practically new, which are cleaned and sent to second-hand shops in Germany; items that are worn but in decent condition which are cleaned and sent to wholesalers around the world; and rags which are used to make recycled paper. Different items are reserved for specific regions: shirts, t-shirts, trousers, children's clothing and household textiles are sent to Africa. Warmer clothes, like coats, jumpers and trousers are sent to Eastern Europe.

"It sounds like a great business model," I say.

"That's what most people think!" says the boss. "Apart from the fee we pay to the charity we get the clothes for practically nothing – so it can be a pretty good business. But these days, at least half of the clothes are only good for export – so the business doesn't make its money back."

"How come? I ask.

"There's a lot of competition and the costs are high. The containers have to be emptied regularly – and the sorting process is labour intensive. A machine can't do it . . ."

I'm so deep in conversation with him that I stop paying attention to the sorting process going on around me. This is why I miss the moment when a worker on my left pulls my red fleece out of her pile. While she inspects it a bit more closely, she listens in to our conversation.

". . . it's too expensive for most clothing recyclers to continue working in Europe," the boss goes on.

"So what do they do?"

"Well, they stick all the unsorted clothes in containers and ship them to Dubai. There, immigrant workers from India, Pakistan, Indonesia and Africa do the work for about $300 US dollars a month," he tells me.

"And that's how companies save money?"

"In Dubai they don't have to pay even a fifth of the wage that is required by law in Europe," he explains.

The worker on my left is so intent on listening in on what we're talking about that she overlooks the stain on my fleece. Seconds later, it finds itself in a container bound for Africa. I head home two hours later. My fleece is in a huge compactor along with 50 other pieces of clothing. The clothes are squashed together into a big ball, wrapped in plastic and kept compressed with industrial rubber bands.

The small but heavy bundles are transported by wheelbarrow to the waiting container in the yard. It takes another two days of sorting and compacting until the container for Africa is filled.

9 November 2007

Early in the morning, a truck backs up into the company's yard. The container is loaded onto the truck by forklift, and away it goes. If the fleece had a window seat, it would say, "Hey, I know this road!" The truck is heading north on the motorway to the container port in Hamburg.

8

The Fishing Industry and People Trafficking: A Journey to West Africa

13 November 2007

Wilfried Hermann, the crane driver, feels a jerk as he lifts up the recycled clothing container. The container has been sitting in Hamburg port for four days now which is much longer than most of the other containers, which have already come and gone. In the meantime many large container freighters have docked in the quay, but these are all headed towards Asia or America. Ships heading in the direction of West Africa only come by once or twice a week.

The container is placed into the belly of the *Hannover* – a combined passenger and container ship that regularly sails the West African route (the Canaries, Dakar, Lagos, Cape Town). Wilfried Hermann has to unload the ship before reloading it again, and as he does he notes to himself the main difference between the freight heading to Asia and freight heading to Africa: ships heading to Asia sail with more empty containers than full ones. However, it's the exact opposite for the ones heading to Africa. Lots of full containers are sent to Africa and then come back empty. This illustrates the fact that Africa, aside from its limited oil resources, is not a big player in the globalised world of today. The *Hannover* sets off late in the afternoon. It sails back down the River Elbe until it reaches the North German port of Cuxhaven, then across the North Sea and the English Channel, and finally heads south along the Western European coast.

14 November 2007

As the ship passes through the English Channel, engineer Karl Hartmann heads out on deck with a pair of binoculars and looks out to sea. Karl is a 'Duck Spotter'. He's looking for ducks bobbing about in the water – a popular hobby for many people who spend lots of time at sea. 'Duck Spotting' began in January 1992, when a freighter lost a couple of containers in the middle of the Pacific Ocean during a storm. One of the containers opened and about 29,000 plastic ducks, beavers, turtles and frogs floated up to the surface. The majority of them drifted south and washed up on the Indonesian and South American coast, and around 10,000 headed northwards through the Bering Sea's Arctic waters. Sometime in 1995, many of the plastic creatures became frozen in ice. Six years later, near Greenland, they were released when the ice melted and floated into the middle of the Atlantic Ocean. The Gulf Stream then sent them towards Great Britain and the Iberian Peninsula.

These unsinkable plastic specimens, bleached by the sun and the saltwater, can be identified by the 'First Years' branding stamped into the plastic. If *you* happen to find one, contact Curtis Ebbesmeyer. For him they are invaluable objects, whose journeys can tell us a lot about global ocean currents. Curtis Ebbesmeyer has even set up a website dedicated to tracking global flotsam: **https://beachcombersalert.org/ RubberDuckies.html**. As well as plastic ducks, the site reports on trainers, glass balls, and the eggs of the mysterious elephant bird.

16 November 2007

Ten hours ago, the *Hannover* left the northern Spanish port of Bilbao carrying both passengers and containers bound for the Canary Islands. The ship sailed south, parallel to the coast of the Iberian Peninsula, until it reached the Strait of Gibraltar (which is approximately 60 kilometres long). The strait joins the Mediterranean Sea to the Atlantic Ocean. On a clear day you can see the coast of Africa from Gibraltar; at this point

Europe and Africa are only separated by 14 kilometres of water. At no other point on the planet does the world of the poor and the world of the rich come into such close proximity. When the weather is good you can also see Europe from the Moroccan coast, which for many Africans is a longed-for paradise.

Today, however, everything is hidden in mist. This means that the passengers don't notice the ship taking a slightly south-westerly course towards Las Palmas of Gran Canaria, the capital of the Canary Islands. Geographically, the Canaries belong to Africa and not to Europe. However, over the course of the last 500 years, so many Spaniards have settled on these islands that they have become a European outpost. A desirable outpost too; all ships heading for America used to stop here first before sailing across the Atlantic. Nowadays, the islands offer visitors 'a slice of Europe' with an African climate – sunshine all year round.

18 November 2007

Having delivered and received passengers, the *Hannover* leaves Las Palmas and heads towards the south-west coast of Africa. It's now on course for Dakar, the capital of Senegal. Engineer Karl hasn't found any plastic ducks on this journey. However, that afternoon the officer on duty spots something else that catches his eye, something dangerous: 'nutshells'.

Nutshells are small, wooden fishing boats filled with African refugees, often found floating off into open seas in hope of reaching the Canary Islands. The officer informs the captain of this news.

For captains of ships that take the same routes as refugees, these encounters are often complicated. Not only is the captain obliged to help people in distress at sea, he also *wants* to help them. But he knows that doing so could cause problems for all parties involved. He asks himself: *Do the refugees need help or would they rather be left alone?* If he takes them aboard in international waters, there will be the difficult question of where they can disembark. No country is obligated to take refugees. Almost every captain has heard tales of ships taking refugees aboard only to discover that the refugees are simply not welcome *anywhere*. The refugees will be angry if they're left in the wrong country, and the shipping companies will be anything but pleased if there's a hold up in the schedule as it will cost them hundreds of thousands of euros.

However, by the time the captain arrives on the bridge the boat can no longer be spotted with a pair of binoculars and the refugees aren't responding to radio contact. The captain can see from the radar, however, that they are on course for the Canaries. No rescue is needed, this time. The captain breathes a sigh of relief and announces, "Steady as she goes."

20 November 2007

The *Hannover* has reached the coast of Senegal which sticks out into the sea like a nose. On its outermost tip is the capital, Dakar, with its suburbs, international airport and fishing village complete with beachside hotels. In the bay, which is on the route to Dakar's harbour, is the 1,000 metre long island of Gorée. Gorée is known as the 'Island of Slaves' and was named by UNESCO (the United Nations Educational, Scientific and Cultural Organisation) as a 'World Heritage Site'. Slaves were once shipped abroad from this island. The 'Slave House', a round building painted pink in the centre of the island, is still visible from a distance. There's a small opening in the wall of the building, which became famously known as the 'Door of No Return'. The Africans who went through it never saw their homes again. After being locked in small cells for a week they would be squeezed like livestock onto ships. It was well known that many would die on the transatlantic journey from illness, hunger and thirst. The cane sugar and tobacco plantations in South America and the Caribbean needed workers who could toil in immense heat. Between the 15th and 19th centuries, somewhere between 10 and 50 million Africans were abducted from their homes in the first and most cruel wave of globalisation of modern times.

Senegal: Poor Country, Rich Country

Like many West African countries, Senegal is a fairly poor country due to a recent and dramatic population increase. The population has doubled in the last 20 years, so around half of the 12 million Senegalese citizens are less than 20 years old and two thirds of them can neither read nor write. Poor nourishment and a shortage of medical care contribute to the reason why, on average, men only live until they're 55 and women until they're 57.

Senegal is located in the Sahel region, the place between the Sahara desert in the North and the Sudanian savannah of the South. A large part of this land is dry savannah – only 16 per cent of the area is fertile, and unfortunately this land is poorly used. Although two thirds of the population work on the land, Senegal cannot produce even half of the food its people need.

Why is this? For 300 years Senegal was a French colony and only gained its independence in 1960. Like most African countries during the colonial period, Senegal was forced to produce very specific products for export. In Senegal these were predominantly peanuts and cotton, which are still produced in large quantities today. The price of these products on the world market has fallen dramatically over the last decade because the USA provides huge financial support to its own cotton and peanut farms (and the EU does exactly the same thing within other areas of agriculture). Because of this, only 20 per cent of national wealth in Senegal comes from farming.

Many Senegalese have moved from the countryside to the cities to try and escape the growing poverty and desperation in the rural areas. As work is also hard to come by in the cities, most people have to get by selling whatever they can: food, lottery tickets, furniture, souvenirs for tourists, clothes and so on. Yet Senegal also has some of the best-developed road networks in Africa. Furthermore, the harbour in Dakar is the second largest and one of the most modern in West Africa. Surrounding the harbour are thriving sugar, vegetable oil, fish and textile industries.

21 November 2007

A crane lifts 40 to 50 containers onto the dockside at Dakar harbour. Everything is more chaotic here than the container harbours of Hamburg and Singapore. Here, the cranes grab containers and put them wherever there is a free space, with very little forward planning.

It's often said that globalisation exploits developing countries – particularly those in Africa. Many people are still under the impression that Africans have the majority of what they produce taken away from them, just like in the 19th and early 20th centuries. At this time Africa was the world's greatest exporter of raw materials, spices and exotic goods, and the large industrialised nations of the West fought to colonise it. These days, the opposite is true: dozens of full containers are unloaded from the ships that arrive there and very few full ones are returned. Sometimes, even empty containers are loaded back onto the ships, because there's no container storage space left at the harbour.

Is this exploitation? This depends on which products are being transported. It's not only old clothes from Europe that are flooding into Africa. On the dockside are also hundreds of old cars which have been shipped from Europe to Africa. Other containers are loaded with food, for example, onions from Holland, beef from Germany and so on. All of these products come from rich countries and have been on very long journeys. Nevertheless, they are sold in Senegal for way below their cost price. The Senegalese buy these products because they are cheap, which means the local farmers who produce food in Senegal barely earn anything. All of this food, which has been shipped in these containers has been heavily subsidised by the European Union. This means that the EU pays its farmers for every onion and pint of milk, which makes it possible for the food to be sold so cheaply in Africa.

The receiver of the old clothing container waits at the entrance to the harbour: Moustapha received the paperwork for the shipment by fax from Hamburg and has come immediately to pick it up. He's brought all the paperwork with him, but the harbour manager informs him that unfortunately his container doesn't seem to be there.

Disappointed, Moustapha heads back to the pick-up truck and tells the driver to wait while he heads back to his office to call Hamburg. In Hamburg they tell him that the container *has* to be there.

22 November 2007

First thing the next morning, Moustapha goes looking for the container. He studies the markings on the side of each metal box trying to find the one that belongs to him. Eventually, after half an hour in the unbearable heat, he finds it. He goes back to the harbour offices, and sure enough, his container's details still aren't on the harbour's received freight list.

After much pleading, one of the harbour managers agrees to go to the spot where the container is.

"Well I'll be damned! It's like magic! It really is here!" the manager exclaims.

However, the manager's original feelings of relief quickly change to confusion. The container shouldn't be here as it's not on their list. He decideds to speak to his colleagues about the situation. After 30 minutes the manager returns and tells Moustapha, "This is a big problem. We need to speak with the Ministry of Trade." Moustapha can't take any more. He takes one of the customs officers to a quiet corner. They speak quickly – hands are raised over and over and they both sigh many times in frustration. Eventually, as in Bangladesh, a small envelope changes hands . . .

When they finally return, everything's been sorted out. The problem with the list is suddenly no longer important and tomorrow the container will magically appear on the list. Two hours later a crane will then load the container onto the truck that's been waiting since yesterday.

They can finally get going – but now the pick-up truck won't start. Moustapha looks at the driver, who shrugs his shoulders. "It was working yesterday," he mutters. A stranger leans into the cab. "Do you want me to go get some petrol? I have a bike and I'm as fast as the wind!"

The driver waves him away. He picks up a hammer, climbs out of the truck and opens the bonnet. The truck is immediately surrounded by men. As long as you're not in the Sahara, you're never alone in Africa. The men give out advice and make jokes while they wait for the moment they can help someone load or unload a truck. That way they can earn a few CFA francs (CFA is the abbreviation for Senegal's currency: franc de la Communauté Financière Africaine) – though they'd prefer euros. The driver hits the engine here and there with the hammer, fiddles with the piston rings and curses loudly.

"Shall I go and get some petrol?" one of the men asks.

"Get lost!" snaps the driver.

After half an hour he finds the problem: the petrol tank is empty. The driver had left the car running with the air conditioning on because it was so hot. Three men fight over the petrol can. One of them is victorious and gets his friend – the one with the bike – to take them to the next petrol station. A quarter of an hour later they're back with the petrol.

Finally, the driver and Moustapha can leave. They drive through the capital at a snail's pace: vans, buses, trucks, cyclists, mopeds *and* a crowd of people are clogging up the road. This means that we have plenty of time to take a look around.

Dakar has around two million inhabitants – making it about the same size as Hamburg (or twice the size of

Birmingham in the UK). The city appears to have been cobbled together without much forward planning. High-rise blocks tower over mud huts, while stylish hotels, bars and shops stand next to shacks made out of plywood and corrugated iron. Thousands of colourful handkerchiefs flutter between buildings: the Senegalese may be quite poor, but life here is loud, fun and colourful. They love music; you can hear it everywhere on the streets, from Caribbean dancehall to salsa. Above all however, there is an African mix of funk and pop, known as 'mbalax', which was made famous by Senegalese musicians Youssou N'Dour and Omar Pene. Like all Africans, the Senegalese also love vivid colours, especially the women who wear colourful clothing or traditional robes called boubous which are covered in vivid patterns. The men cover their cars, fishing boats, signs above their shops and whatever else is important to them with colourful patterns too. There are a lot of horns sounding on the roads today – everybody wants everyone else to get out of the way because they think they're in the biggest rush!

Moustapha's place is on a side street just off Avenue G. Pompidou. It's only 1.5 kilometres away from the harbour, but it's taken over half an hour to get here. The truck parks in front of a huge doorway. The driver hasn't opened the doors of the container yet as there's a group of men hanging around in the hope that they'll be asked to unload the truck. Moustapha doesn't have any employees.

In Africa, especially in the cities, there are always a couple of men in the area 'by chance' who are willing to either unload or load something. Moustapha haggles with the men over how much he's willing to pay them to unload the truck. They agree on 2,500 CFA francs, which is around €40 euros. After they've carried the second bundle of clothing into the building on their shoulders, the men are sweating so much that their faces begin to shine. They are closely supervised by an associate of Moustafa, who keeps track of how many bundles of clothing they have carried on a piece of paper. This piece of paper won't be kept for Moustapha's records, it's just a way of making it clear to the workers that they are being watched, so nothing goes missing during the unloading process.

The bundles of clothing won't be in Moustapha's possession for long. News of the arrival of new merchandise has spread like wildfire, and curious locals have flocked to check it out. But the problem with the bundles of clothing is that there are 'good' bundles, and there are 'bad' bundles. In good bundles you can find 10 or 20 good pairs of stonewashed jeans with frayed legs. But in bad bundles, there is only clothing made from linen – trousers made of thick cloth and shirts in boring colours. People only want to buy the good bundles – but the challenge is to work out which are good and which are bad. No one is allowed to open up any of the bundles – otherwise everyone would look through them and only take the good stuff. From the outside, it's very hard to tell which of the bundles are good. Africans are very fashion conscious, just like Europeans. The young Senegalese find out what is popular in more developed countries through adverts in newspapers, films or online. No one wants to buy light blue jeans from the second hand shop – they'd rather have no jeans at all!

Cotton, Boubous and Why Africa is Losing its Colour

When we think of Africa we think of the Serengeti with its elephants, lions and wildebeest, and above all a boisterous mixture of people wearing colourful clothes. Two out of every three items of clothing in Africa are the product of clothes recycling. Thousands of tonnes of old clothes are brought from Europe every year to West Africa. East Africa gets most of its recycled clothing from North America. These imported clothes actually cause many problems for the people who live in Africa. The clothing is sold even more cheaply than the clothing produced locally in West Africa. A lot of people would have worked hard to produce these traditional clothes: from growing the cotton and spinning the thread, to sewing the items. In Ghana it's completely different: here, people only buy clothes that have been made in the country. In Mali the boubou is a status symbol. It's a long, celebratory robe with fine embroidery – and it's produced in West Africa.

Among the people looking at the clothing bundles is Aisha, a 38-year-old mother of five who owns a market stall in northern St. Louis. Aisha got up at 4.00am this morning to get to Dakar to buy clothes for her stall. She's looking for bundles, which through the packaging, seem to have more blue and bright red as hopefully these bundles will contain jeans and colourful dresses, which have been selling well lately. Aisha has to pay 80,000 CFA francs for her bundles, which is around €120 euros.

A boy accompanies Aisha – fifteen year old Mohammed. He won't leave her side for the whole day and takes care of all the heavy lifting. Mohammed carries the bundles to the bus station, the Gare Routieres de Pompiers, near the Grand Mosque, to where the 'taxi-brousse' are parked (the 'bus-taxis'). These minibuses only have 12 actual seats, but the drivers make extra, makeshift seats out of wood, folding benches or simple metal rods. That way, with a bit of pushing and squeezing about 30 people can fit inside. The minibus won't leave until it's full, and it takes two hours to squash enough passengers into the bus to fill it. No one can turn or lift their arms, and Aisha and Mohammed sit in silence, sweating. *Why isn't the bus moving?* A man appears at the driver's window and gives him a package. There is much talking and gesturing, which they hope is the signal to leave! The driver starts the minibus's engine, zooms on to the main road without looking right or left, and heads north.

Everyone enjoys the air that streams in through the open windows, but they only get to enjoy it for a moment as the heavy traffic makes them keep stopping. As soon as the traffic allows, the driver hits the accelerator. It seems that he wants to make up for all the time he spent waiting at the bus station. The passengers are shaken our of their seats, and those sitting close to the windows start to fear for their lives.

Mohammed whispers a prayer for protection. Aisha on the other hand is familiar with this journey. She sits sideways so she can always see the back of the bus. The worst thing for her would be if one of her bundles fell off the back.

23 November 2007

Created by French colonists, the port town of St. Louis is the Venice of West Africa. The centre of the city is situated on a long island between the river Senegal and the sea, joined to the mainland by a 500 metre long bridge. The bridge's curved arches, made by French engineer Gustave Eiffel, were made from the same steel he used to build his famous tower in Paris. The old city centre consists of tightly packed, stone colonial houses, which are becoming more and more run down. Aisha lives here with her family.

After a bumpy 10 hour journey with one bus change, Aisha, Mohammed and the bundles make it home in the early hours of the morning. Aisha will open up the bundles and lay out her new wares on her market stall by the beach. She does some calculations in her head. The bundles cost €120 euros each. Her family need around €120 euros to survive for two weeks, so she needs to make at least €240 euros. She usually meets her target, but not always. Sometimes, smaller traders like Aisha buy a dud bundle. A couple of weeks ago, she got a bundle that only made €100 euros, so it didn't even cover the cost price. In Africa, it's not possible to get refunds for bad products. People are used to getting by on strokes of good or bad luck and instead of moaning about it, they try to find other ways to make ends meet.

3 December 2007

There are lots of wooden fishing boats on the beach at St. Louis. Most of them are elaborately painted and have whimsical names like *Gift of God* or *Merciful Heart*. Tourists are always stopping to photograph them. The beach looks especially beautiful when the fishermen return with their catch. The beaches overflow with people when this happens because everyone wants some delicious fresh fish. However this scenic picture is deceptive; the fishermen only used to have to go to sea for one or two days. They would then be forced to return as their ships were so loaded down with fish. Nowadays, even after a whole week at sea the catch is *still* poor. Huge commercial trawlers are to blame for this – they take the fish from right under the fishermen's noses.

Among the people on the beach is 18-year-old Adrame. He comes from a small inland village where there's been virtually no work for many years: cotton can't be grown as there's too little water and growing peanuts is no longer profitable.

West Africa and Europe: A History of Suffering

Fishermen often end up selling their boats to human traffickers because they can no longer make a living from fishing. This is largely the fault of European trawlers – these trawlers depend on the fish on the West African coast. The European Union has provided around four billion euros to boost the fishing sector. Much of this money was used to buy the rights to fish off the West African coast. The money didn't go to the local West African fishermen however, but into the Senegalese government's pockets. The EU funding *should* have been used to protect jobs, but instead the money was used by commercial fishing companies to buy bigger and more powerful boats. Often the West Africans who work on the European ships do so for low wages, especially the Spanish trawlers. In short: West Africans are being exploited with help from EU funding, and are having their livelihood destroyed at the same time.

Due to much criticism from the media, the EU have now placed much stronger constraints on European fishermen: they can no longer take so many fish from the West African coast, and have to use looser nets so the younger fish don't get caught. The aim of this was to protect coastal fishing for the West Africans. The Senegalese government promptly sold the fishing rights for even more money to Korea – without *any* protection for the Senegalese fishermen.

Adrame spent some time in Dakar, but he was only able to get small odd jobs here and there. He has no relatives in Dakar and doesn't know anyone there either, which is what you need to get a job. That's why he wants to go to Europe. In fact, Adrame wants to go to Europe more than anything, mainly because his old school friend Adbouleyle told him what it's like. Adbouleyle has done really well there. He came back to visit his old village about six months ago. He was well dressed and had a huge watch, big sunglasses and a white woman at his side. The woman was his new wife.

"When you first get there everything's so easy!" his friend told him when they were alone. "You can get a permanent job. I work in a restaurant called McDonald's; it's the largest restaurant chain in the world. Do you get me?" He pinched Adame's side. "It is pretty cold there, but you can afford all the clothes in the world. You see something and then you just buy it! No more second-hand clothes for me."

After his friend had left again, Adame couldn't stop thinking about what he'd been told. Dakar was no longer his goal, he wanted to go to Europe; he wanted to be in paradise just like his friend. For days he's been looking for a boat that will take him to the Canary Islands. He's stopped caring how big or how old the boat is that takes him, or even how many people are on the boat. The only thing that matters is that he has the €350 euros for the journey over, which he had great difficulty borrowing from family and friends.

The skipper beckons Adame over, and tells him it costs €500 to €600 euros per place on the boat. The skipper has to buy the boat from the fisherman and he needs to hire an experienced sailor. He also needs to pay for the petrol. On top of this, the many contacts he has looking for immigrants to fill the boat will also want payment.

7 December 2007

As Adrame wanders through the town looking for a ride he hears a lot of terrible things about the journey to the so-called European 'paradise'. For the last few days radio announcements, made by the government, have been being playing day and night: "Your dreams will not come true!" he hears, over and over. What these messages are trying to say is that most refugees will never make it to Europe. They drown or are deported. If they do make it, they are treated as illegal immigrants. They must work in horrible jobs, are badly paid and can't even visit a doctor when they get sick. But the people on the beach say: "The Europeans pay for those radio announcements!" Today in the café someone told Adrame that the government has allowed European aeroplanes, helicopters and speedboats with machine guns to patrol the borders to international waters. They tip the boats over and then they shoot everyone inside them.

"Rubbish!" someone calls out. "You don't really believe that our government would let foreigners kill us?"

"Our government cannot be trusted!" replies a third person, "they would have us all sold as slaves if someone would pay for us!'

This was followed by a long silence. Suddenly everyone felt insignificant and defenceless.

Adrame manages to ignore all of these comments but then he hears something he cannot get out of his head. Many ships are damaged during storms or go round in circles because they've lost their way. In the most dire situations, the boats capsize and everyone on board drowns – then their bodies wash up on the coast of Morocco.

That *can't* happen to Adrame. He decides that he will visit a mage – also called a marabout.

The people of Senegal are Muslim, but many of their ancient rites and spiritual beliefs date from the pre-Muslim era. These beliefs are inspired by nature; that there are good and bad spirits everywhere, but only marabouts can see them. If a good spirit hovers above a person or a journey then everything will be fine. If a bad spirit is present, then a marabout might be able to help you. If he is not successful though, you should give up your plans. Adrame haggles with the marabout for a long time. Money exchanges hands, and then the marabout seeks advice from his ancestors and his invisible helpers. He drinks a strange liquid from a bottle, sways backwards and forwards and his eyes begin to roll back in his head.

He blesses Adrame with a magical spell, places his hands on Adrame's head and sprays a little liquid into his face. Finally, the marabout murmurs words Adrame can barely understand: "You will . . . reach . . . your goal – but . . . beware . . . long . . . shadow over your boat . . . they are following you . . . protection . . . something that glows . . ."

Protection . . . something that glows? Adrame wants to ask what exactly the marabout means, but the marabout awakens slowly from his trance and simply says: "Go now, I am weary!"

Should Adrame protect himself with something that glows? Or should he protect himself *from* something that glows? For half an hour, Adrame wanders through the town until he sees the red fleece body warmer at Aisha's stall – perhaps this is a sign.

Sounding a little naive, he says to the stall owner: "It looks magical!"

"Yes," she says, "it's made from a water-resistant material. Water cannot get through it and you don't sweat in it. This body warmer really does have magical powers . . . If I really think about it, 150 francs is too cheap."

Adrame has to question this: "Why hasn't anyone bought it yet then? Maybe there's a curse on it. It doesn't even really look that good." Adrame unfolds the body warmer.

"Hey, there's a huge stain on it!"

"Okay, 130 francs!" Aisha says quickly "Discounted price. Give me the money!"

And the red fleece finally changes hands.

9

Some are Thirsty, Others are Not: A Showdown in Tenerife

14 December 2007

At sunset, the refugees assemble on the beach. Today should be the day that they finally set off on their long jouney. After his €350 euros has been rejected countless times, the skipper finally accepts the money. "Don't expect any luxuries. That's just about enough for the boat and the petrol." The skipper looks devious. For a few days, nothing happens. Adrame comes to the beach every afternoon and looks for the skipper, but he is always told: "Not today! Maybe tomorrow." Twice the refugees have all gathered at the beach expecting to leave, but the skipper thought the weather was too poor. If the waves are higher than two metres, an open boat stands no chance.

Today's the day. The skipper collects all the money. He also takes everyone's passports and documentation, so he can burn them. "Is that everyone's papers? If there's a single document on board, we'll all be sent back. If they catch you in international waters, you can't have any papers on you. Say your name, but not where you come from. That way, they can't send you back to Senegal. They're not allowed to. Whatever happens in the next few hours, keep your mouth shut. We have to make it to international waters!"

Adrame's friend had told him to check over the whole boat. Are there any holes in it? Has it got a good motor and enough petrol? Does it have a navigation system on board so they can find their way? But how can Adrame find all this out? It's dark, and they're led onto the boat at the last minute. The skipper looks mean and has a huge knife sticking out of his waistband. Adrame has paid a cheap price for the journey. If he asks any questions, he's sure that he'll be thrown off the boat and won't get his money back. So Adrame doesn't take a close look at the boat before he climbs on board, and instead squeezes in amongst the other 62 refugees. He sits at the front of the boat, which isn't a good spot but for the price he's paid he can't complain. As the boat makes its way through the surf, everyone at the front gets wet. Adrame's wearing the red fleece body warmer.

How Can a Senegalese Person Make it to Europe?

There are three ways in which a Senegalese person might successfully make it to Europe:

1. The safest method is to marry a European. But how does a Senegalese person find a European to marry? Very few tourists come to Senegal looking for marriage. So, to find a European to marry, you have to be in Europe.

2. The cheapest route is not to take a fishing boat, but to go by aeroplane. A ticket from Dakar to Paris costs around €300 euros, but you'll also need a visa. A fake visa will get you past the customs officials in Dakar, but once you get to Paris you'll be found out and flown straight back.

3. The most dangerous and most expensive method is to cross the Atlantic Ocean in an open boat by paying human traffickers to take you into Europe illegally.

Up until 2006, the main route for African refugees was through the Strait of Gibraltar towards Spain. It went straight through the Sahara to the Moroccan coast, so a lot of the journey was on foot. But since 2006 this route has been more strictly patrolled and the Moroccans come down hard on illegal immigrants. So now the new routes go around Morocco. The eastern route runs through Libya, across the Mediterranean towards Italy or Greece, and the western route runs along the Mauritian or Senegalese coast and across the open Atlantic to the Canary Islands.

These journeys last four or five days and cost around €600 euros. The price depends on the relative safety and comfort of the ship: are the boats made from wood or steel? Are they motorised and do they have a navigation system on board and so on. The young Senegalese used to have to rely on word of mouth from friends and families to discover the answer to these questions, but now they can learn a lot from the Internet. People trafficking 'tours' are offered alongside 'normal' trips. You can see the weather forecast for the Atlantic on the Internet too: which direction is the wind blowing? Will storms be brewing in the next few days, or will the Harmattan, a wind that carries sand from the Sahara, make it impossible to see? However those who are trying to prevent people trafficking have upgraded too: The European Union have founded the border defence organisation Frontex, which patrols the West African coast with reconnaissance planes, helicopters and boats so that they can prevent refugees from entering international waters.

Adrame uses his 'magical fleece' to keep dry when the water splashes into the boat over and over again. They've barely left the shore when the boat driver gives some further instructions: "Anyone caught stealing money or drinking water will be thrown overboard. Only drink one cup of water in the morning and one in the evening, otherwise our supplies won't last and you'll have to wee too often. You have to wee and do your other business over the side of the boat. Get your neighbour to hold on to you so that you don't fall out of the boat. Don't wee into the wind, do it at the back of the boat. With Allah's help, we will make it."

15 December 2007

By sunset Adrame can no longer see the coast. They are completely surrounded by water as far as the eye can see. This is an extraordinary feeling. Adrame looks around him on the boat and he can see lots of young men and a few young women. An old man sits close by. He is 53 years old, and the many traumas and disappointments of his life have left behind deep furrows and lines on his face. Why is an old man making such a difficult journey? "Why are you here?" Adrame asks the man.

"You know, everyone thinks that I'm too old, that I won't make it. But I've been through more than all of you put together. I've worked for 40 years and have survived a famine. All my children now live in the promised land, in France. My wife died of yellow fever last year. No doctors would visit us. That would never have happened in France. The loneliness I feel every morning when I wake up is like a terrible illness. Every evening when I go to bed alone feels like a small death. I have to break free from this life of isolation. If I die on the way to my children, that's fine by me. I have left my life behind. But all of you, you have your whole lives ahead of you. That is why Allah must lead the hand of our boat driver . . ."

16 December 2007

"There!" Adrame calls out.

"There's something there!" his neighbour says.

"No, there's nothing there. No, no," comes the gentle answer.

Everyone was warned that you start seeing land or high mountains, when they're actually a couple of clouds or the crests of high waves. They're in your imagination. The more exhausted you are, the more incredible the things you see become.

They sing for hours on end. Always the same lilting songs, "Houh-hohoho-houh – soon we will arrive. Houh-hohoho-houh – in beautiful Europe . . ."

Everyone laughs freely. Then some of them sing something more sombre. "Will we see our villages again? What will happen to my parents, who will care for my brothers and sisters? Allah – what have you got planned for us?"

The women begin to cry and the men stare out to sea.

The body warmer protects Adrame from the sea spray and the cold of the night, but it turns out it doesn't stop you from sweating at all. He is extremely hot, and his face has started to burn.

17 December 2007

All night long fishing trawlers sail back and forth. One of them is the *Alhambra* from Spain. First mate Miguel follows large swarms of fish using the radar, but he cannot see small boats. *Those damn fish*, he thinks to himself, *one minute they're here, the next they're over there, then they dive out of reach or they're in the shallows near the coast.*

Suddenly Miguel spots a huge swarm in his sights. They could be sardines! Miguel quickly changes course and in doing so heads straight towards Adrame's refugee boat. The boat full of people appears in front of him as if from nowhere. Miguel looks up at the exact moment the first ray of sunlight hits the sea. He sees something red like a buoy in the distance. Watch out! Miguel turns the rudder. This tiny change in course means the trawler misses the refugee boat by just a few metres. As the trawler sails past the boat, Miguel can see that there's no light on the front of the refugee boat's hull.

"These damn Africans!" Miguel screams. Then he looks at the people crammed on board the tiny fishing boat. Oh, more poor people who've sold their souls! Miguel crosses himself and regrets cursing. He thanks the Holy Mary for being born a Spaniard. The Senegalese and Mauritian workers at the back of the trawler working the nets forget their work for a moment. There is silence as the Africans on board the trawler look at the Africans on board the refugee boat.

They don't greet each other, no one says a word. Why would they? There's nothing to say. The men working on the fishing trawler have already made the hardest journey of their lives, and they know all too well that many of the refugees will pay with their lives. In spite of this, there is no way that any of them would try to change the refugees' minds.

The refugees look at their fellow countrymen working like slaves. They think to themselves: *If I make it through this journey, I will never step on a boat again, and definitely not a trawler working in all sorts of weather conditions.* The men on the trawler know that this is what the refugees are thinking. But they know better: when you're actually in Europe, it's completely different to how it's talked about at home. You can't get a proper job without papers. Maybe you'll manage to find work on a farm during harvest time, but on a trawler you'll have your own bunk and a secure job that brings you no trouble. As the men and women think these thoughts, the refugee boat is lost in the semi-darkness. The workers on the boat look at one another. Slowly, they start working again.

18 December 2007

For four days they've had virtually nothing to eat, and the drinking water was used up 48 hours ago. Adrame is so weak that he can barely see, and his bones have begun to hurt from sitting in one position for such a long time. The old man is the only one who doesn't complain. "I worked for forty years. I did everything. There's not a dirty job that I haven't done, except be an executioner or a state president. Now I'm seeing the world – sitting down. Wonderful."

Adrame has the sinking feeling that the boat driver has lost his way. He only lets the motor run for about an hour a day and tries to tell the direction the current is moving by hand.

Sometime later, the old man becomes contemplative too: "Adrame, you have to promise me two things in case my journey ends sooner than yours. Here is my lucky charm, an amulet I wear around my neck, take it. Perhaps you will find my children and you can give it to them. Or you can give it to your children. Inside this bag are my festive clothes. I want to wear them when you release me into the sea and I drift amongst the dolphins and the whales . . . Can you promise me that?"

"Yes," Adrame whispers. He cannot say anything more.

Date Unknown, December 2007

Have they been travelling for four or six days? Adrame cannot be sure. He doesn't care anymore. His bottom hurts terribly. He's so squeezed into his spot on the boat that he cannot shift his weight from one side to the other. Strangely, he doesn't feel hungry, but his throat is so dry it burns. There hasn't been any drinking water for a very long time. Millions of litres of water slosh around them – saltwater. His mouth is so dry that he can't feel his tongue anymore. At one point he came close to chewing it off. They should be there by now. The journey should only have lasted four days. The driver hasn't used the motor since the night before. Presumably there's no more petrol, but no one dares to ask. Every now and then, someone starts moaning or complaining but for the most part, the boat is silent.

21 December 2007

Finally, a holiday! Steve Miller from England lies back on his sun lounger on one of Tenerife's glorious beaches. He doesn't get to go on holiday very often. But once a year, he and his wife indulge in a couple of days of sun, sea and sand. As it's just before Christmas there's only one place in Europe that is warm enough for a beach holiday: the Canary Islands.

Last night's quick trip to the hotel bar turned into a long one. At some point in the evening he managed to make his way back to his hotel room. His wife took no pity on him, and woke him up shortly after 9:00am. "Come on, get up, otherwise we'll miss breakfast! You can sleep on the beach all day!"

"I'm going to bed early tonight," he moans. That afternoon Steve sleeps for three long hours on his sun lounger on the beach.

At the same time, 60 kilometres away, the refugees are feeling dispirited. Their faces are burnt and they are too weak from thirst and hunger to moan or complain. For the last few hours Adrame has wondered if the old man is still alive. He hasn't moved for some time. He hasn't even sighed. Do old, exhausted people move in their sleep? He doesn't want to disturb him. If he's only sleeping he doesn't want to wake him, and if he is dead, he can no longer help him. And then he sees something on the horizon. But he knows that they are only cursed waves and cursed clouds and cursed spirits leading him astray.

22 December 2007

Steve falls on to his sun lounger and lets out a sigh. Today he feels *much* better. The sea lies before him and his wife, his crime novel and his sun cream are next to him on the hot sand. He paddles in the waves for a little while and then lies back down. He doesn't make it very far through his novel and falls asleep after one chapter. Later on he lays the book down next to him and looks out at the horizon. There is only dark blue water ahead of him: an endless expanse of sea, with rippling white-capped waves. Once again he goes for a swim, reads a page or two of his novel, dozes, and then has a look around. At some point in the afternoon he notices a dot on the horizon. It's a boat.

He shakes his head, sits up and takes another look. The boat is still there – it's coming slowly towards them, and seems to be being propelled by something. He can only make out that it's a small, open fishing boat. Perhaps it's a local fisherman returning with the day's catch. A quarter of an hour passes and it's now clear that there are many small dots hovering over the boat.

"You see that boat over there?" his wife says, interrupting his thoughts. "Do you think that it's . . ."

"A boat full of refugees!" he finishes the sentence for her.

The closer the boat comes the more they can see. There's 40, 50, perhaps 60 people sitting in a wooden African boat. In this little nutshell, they have managed to travel across the Atlantic from Africa. The motor has stalled on the boat, and those who still have enough strength are rowing towards the coast with planks of wood. In the meanwhile, everyone else on the beach has seen the boat too. No one's reading or sunbathing anymore – everyone looks tense and anxious, wondering what will happen. Around 50 metres from the beach the surf starts getting heavy, and the boat shakes helplessly in the waves. Some of the refugees jump into the water and begin splashing with their arms, panicking. Maybe they can't even swim!

A few people from the beach jump into the water to help save the choking refugees. Steve has his digital camera with him and, without any further thought, unzips his beach bag and pulls it out. But what he's filming chills him to the bone.

Some of the people on the beach are strong swimmers and succeed in grabbing the panicking refugees under the arms and pulling them out of the water. The first refugees on the beach are huddled together. They haven't even got the energy to celebrate. Their expressions are empty, but their eyes are full of fear: they cannot believe that they have survived. Most of them are shaking from head to toe. The camera zooms in on a very young refugee wearing a red body warmer. He is shaking all over. Nevertheless he kneels and tries to pray. He has his arms stretched partly in front of him and is surely thanking Allah that he has survived.

Gradually, ambulances and the coastguard start to arrive, and the holidaymakers go back to the hotel deep in thought. No one feels like sunbathing or swimming anymore. That evening a man comes into the hotel bar and approaches Steve. "I'm from the BBC. Did you film the refugees this morning? What do you want for the footage?"

"What do I want?"

"Well, I can offer you five hundred pounds for the footage and the rights to show it."

Steve thinks for a minute about what you could buy with £500 pounds, and then answers: "I don't want any money. How about you just buy me a beer instead?"

"Just one? OK, drinks are on me tonight!" says the reporter.

The beer doesn't taste quite right though. Steve wanted to leave the world behind him and relax on this holiday. But even in a place as isolated as the Canary Islands, the problems of the world can still find us.

10

How We Could Change the End of This Story Together

15 March 2008

This evening I have to send the rest of this story to my publisher. There's just about enough time left to check the text for errors and check the layout, and then it will be sent off to the printers. Most publishers don't use local printers anymore. Often, books aren't even printed in the same country, but in Italy, Slovenia, India or China.

So, what happened to Adrame and the red fleece? Before I answer this question, something has to be said – although most of the readers of this book will have already realised what I am about to say. This is a story and not a commentary on actual events. My body warmer did actually exist though. And the places that appear in this story are places I have got to know whilst working as a journalist. I have checked and verified every step of this journey, from the drilling of petroleum and the fabric manufacturing processes in Bangladesh, to the arrival methods of refugees on the Canary Islands. How deep is the entrance to the harbour in Dubai? What's the name of the street in front of the station in Chittagong? How many breaks do workers get in the textile factories of Dhaka? How much is a space on a human trafficker's boat?

In my opinion, this story really *could* have happened. Because I didn't have the time or the money to follow my red fleece around the world for two and a half years, my imagination had to help me out a bit. While writing this story, I always tried to be realistic about each step of the journey and what might happen next.

Let's return to Adrame. What could have happened to him after he reached Tenerife? The Spanish authorities have very little information about individual refugees who have made it to Europe. Even less is reported about them in newspapers and on television. In 2006, no less than 30,000 Africans succeeded in reaching Europe on small fishing boats. By 2011, this number had been reduced to 5,433 people due to the introduction of much tougher border patrols. Despite this, around 450 illegal immigrants enter Spanish territories every month. What happens to them?

Announcements made by the Spanish government and

reports in the Spanish media tell us this much: the refugees that make it alive are either taken to internment camps on the islands, or shipped to camps on the Spanish mainland. They are released after 40 days by order of the Spanish government: they leave as free people in the free world.

However, in order to receive valid documentation that will allow them to stay and work in Spain, they must apply for asylum. They must prove that they are being persecuted in their own countries, otherwise they will not be granted asylum and will be deported. Most of the refugees have left their own countries because of poverty, but poverty is not accepted as official grounds for asylum. For this reason, many refugees dive straight into the underground and instantly become illegal immigrants. They live in dilapidated houses or in self-made shacks in the countryside, and work illegally, without paying taxes or social security, sometimes finding jobs as labourers, kitchen assistants or farm hands in the country. They are much more likely to accept poor wages and working conditions, as any work, at the very least, is better than nothing. They become outlaws – people who have no official documentation to prove who they are.

And what happened to the main protagonist of this book, the red fleece itself? It must have been completely worn out after this ordeal. Perhaps it was once again put in a recycling container to be turned back into raw materials and sent on another trip around the world? More likely, it ended up as landfill or was incinerated. Carbon dioxide, which is very harmful to the environment, would have been released into the atmosphere during the burning process, as the body warmer was made of synthetic, carbon based fibres.

Perhaps Adrame cut off a scrap of the body warmer that helped him to freedom. Maybe he attached it to the old man's amulet. Maybe I will recognise him by this little red snippet of fabric, next time I'm in Tenerife, or Gran Canaria, in Madrid or Barcelona, in Nepal or Marseille, in Hamburg or Hannover. Perhaps Adrame is getting by as a street seller. Depending on the weather he might be selling sunglasses or umbrellas to locals and tourists alike. Where are the sunglasses from? The Far East. They look stylish, but their lenses have no UV protection. The people buying the sunglasses want to look cool, and it seems that low prices are more important than proper eye protection or decent working conditions for the manufacturers. When it rains Adrame sells umbrellas that come from . . . The Far East, of course. They are simple in design and usually break during the first storm they encounter, but when they only cost five euros, you can always buy another one.

Does the story have to end like this? Do people have to

buy cheap and badly made products, produced by people who barely make enough money to survive? No, it *doesn't* have to be this way. We *can* change things. Our job is to persuade our governments to play fair when it comes to trade policy. If we demand that other countries open up their markets and stick to the trading rules, our countries must do the same. *Even* if this means that certain areas become more competitive and possibly suffer as a result. Life may become more difficult for farmers and fishermen, but on a global scale, things will be fairer as a result.

Just as in sport, the questions we face are ones of fairness, justice and equality. What is the value of a football victory if the opposition only had five players instead of eleven? We need to develop fairer trade regulations in the global marketplace. Globalisation means not pretending that we have nothing to do with problems in other continents. In a globalised world, we are all in it together.

As consumers, we must do our homework. We need to recognise that with every action, and with every purchase, we are shaping the world we live in.

When we decide to buy one thing over another, we are also deciding which firms earn the profits, which countries can export more goods, and what kind of working conditions we think are acceptable for the people that make these products.

Many consumers believe that the power to change global trade lies with politicians and businessmen. But this is not the case. Increasingly, consumers hold the power to influence world trade, through the choices we make with our shopping trollies and online baskets.

Take my red fleece for example. I should have asked myself: Where did it come from? How much energy was used to produce it, and how much waste was and will be created because of it? Department stores and chain stores will always supply goods acording to consumer demand. But all too often what the consumers demand are cheap products, which we buy without a thought for the working conditions of the manufacturers or the environment. Could we live without that cool pair of trainers, those fashionable trousers, or that cheep red fleece? We need to ask for products that are socially and ecologically sustainable. If we don't, nothing will ever change. The rich will get richer, and the poor will get even poorer.

My mind is made up: next time I buy something warm to wear in my office, it *will* be another fleece from Bangladesh. But this time it will be one that was made in fair working conditions. And this time it won't be red.

About the Author

Wolfgang Korn studied political science and history and works as a journalist and author in Hannover. He writes for newspapers and magazines (GEO and DIE ZEIT, amongst others). His latest book is *Detectives of the Past: Expeditions into the World of Archaeology* (Bloomsbury Children's Books and Books for Young People, 2007).

This book was translated into English from German by Jen Calleja, a writer and translator based in London.

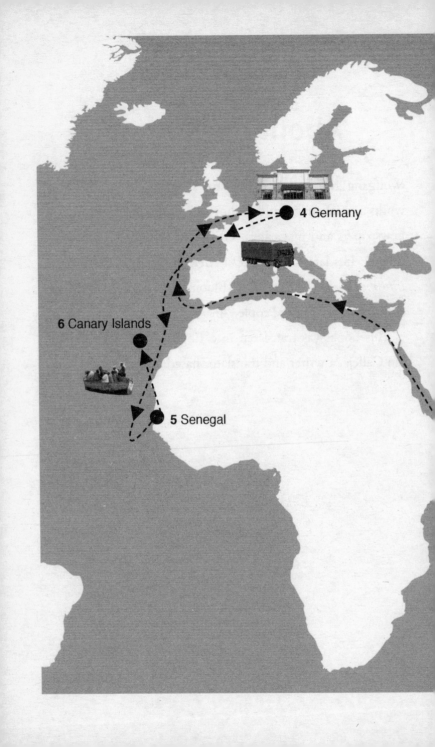

4 Germany

6 Canary Islands

5 Senegal

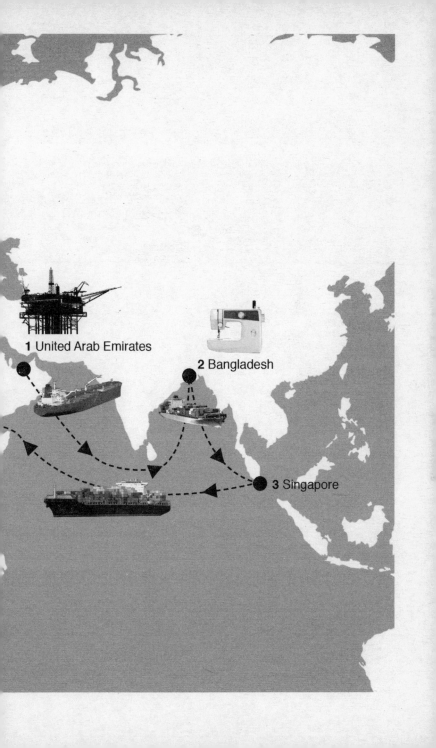

1 United Arab Emirates

2 Bangladesh

3 Singapore

Glossary

abbreviation: short form of a word

advance: payment given to an author before their book goes on sale

antimony: toxic natural element used in medicine and metal compounds

artificial fibre: strand of material created by forcing fibre forming materials through tiny holes
(also see **synthetic fibre**)

Asiatic: Asian

assembly plant: factory where individual parts are assembled into a finished product

asylum: when a government gives a foreigner a safe place to live in their country to protect them from **persecution**

baksheesh: tip or bribe given for a service

ballast tank: tank in a ship that can be filled with water to stabilise the vessel

Baltic region: area surrounding the Baltic Sea

behemoth: large and powerful thing or object

bideshi: Bangladeshi for 'foreigners'

biodegradable waste: also known as **organic waste**, this is waste made of animal or plant matter that can be broken down by bacteria

boisterous: rough and noisy

bolt (of fabric): an industry standard length of material that is stored in a roll (length and width varies according to material)

boubou: a robe worn by West African men and women (both sexes wear boubous in a slightly different manner)

bow: front of a ship

bridge: room or platform from which a ship is commanded

bulk (produce in): to make or produce something in large quantities

canopy: fabric cover held up by poles

coal: a natural form of carbon burned for fuel

commercial: easily made and sold or traded for profit

commodity: product made for trade or buying and selling

consumer: person or group who are final users of products or services

contaminate: when an unwanted or toxic substance is mixed in with another substance

control room: room from which a service or process is controlled

convoy: to travel in a group or line

cost price: how much it costs to make something

counterfeit: fake

crude oil: unrefined oil, also known as **petroleum**

deadweight tonnage (DWT): the maximum weight a ship can safely carry

defenceless: without any form of protection

deftly: skilfully and cleverly

densely populated: a high number of people living in a small area

deported: to be made to leave a country

desalination: to remove salt and other minerals from water

designated: when someone or something is given a particular job

dilapidated: broken and run-down

dire: extremely serious or urgent

disembark: get off a ship

distress (fabric): to give simulated marks of age or wear

domestic (product): commodities produced in a person's home country

dud: failure

echinoderm: invertebrate sea creature

ecologically sustainable: produced in a way that doesn't damage organisms or their environments

economy: the financial state of a country (or region)

elasticity: the ability of an object to return to its original shape after being stretched

ethylene: gas derived from **crude oil** used to make plastics

evaporate: to change from a liquid to a gas

export: products created for trade or sale in other countries

fake goods: products that are illegal copies of designer brand goods

forty foot equivalent unit (FEU): 40 foot long shipping container

flare stack: elevated torch on an oil rig that burns off escaping gas while drilling for crude oil

flotsam: wreckage found floating on water

freight: goods being transported for money

freighter: ship that delivers cargo or goods for money

frond: a large, fine leaf, such as a fern

galley: kitchen area of a ship or an aeroplane

general strike: when people stop working in every **industry** in a town or country as a form of protest

globalisation: the increasingly interlinked nature of the world, in terms of economic relationships, ideas, trade and culture

global warming: increase in the world's overall temperature caused by human activity

Green Dot: a green recycling logo

guthra: cloth headscarf worn by Arab men

Harmattan: a cold and dusty wind that blows across West Africa

hull: the main body of a ship or vessel

imported: brought in from another country

incentive: some kind of reward to encourage a person to do something

inconspicuous: not easily noticed; does not attract attention

industrialised (more-developed) country: a comparatively rich country with a highly developed social, industrial and economic structure

industrial unit: factory or processing plant

illegal immigrant: person who moves to another country without permission

incinerated: burnt to ashes

international waters: bodies of water that don't belong to any one particular country or state

internment camp: a holding centre for prisoners of war or illegal immigrants

intersect: to cut across something else

invertebrate: creature without a spine

jetsam: discarded objects found at sea

kandura: a long robe worn by Arab men

labyrinth: maze

landfill: area of land where rubbish is buried

Large Range 2 (LR2): oil tanker that can carry 80,000-159,000 tonnes of liquid

less-developed (unindustrialised) countries: a comparatively poor country with a less-developed social, industrial and economic structure

list: nautical term for when a ship sits lower in the water on one side than the other

loading bay: area where cargo is loaded and unloaded

loincloth: a piece of cloth worn around the hips as clothing

malleable: able to be flattened or rolled out

mage: (also known as a **marabout**) North African holy man believed to have supernatural powers

mantle: rocky region of the earth's interior between the crust and the core

manufacturer: a person, group or company that runs a manufacturing plant or factory

marabout: (also known as a **mage**) North African holy man believed to have supernatural powers

marketplace: a place where goods and products are sold to the end user, the **consumer**

mass-produced: to produce products in **bulk** in a factory or manufacturing plant

mbalax: genre of popular dance music in Senegal and Gambia

mechanical loom: a machine that weaves fabric

merchandise: goods bought and sold in a business

metaphor: figure of speech in which a word or phrase is not literally applicable

minimum wage: the minimum hourly rate you can be paid for a job by law

molecule: group of atoms bonded together

monsoon season: period of strong winds and heavy rain in Southeast Asia and the Indian Ocean

more-developed (industrialised) countries: a comparatively rich country with a more-developed social, industrial and economic structure

natural gas: gas found trapped in **reservoirs** deep underground

non-perishable: something, usually food, that doesn't go off for a long time

obsolete: no longer produced or used

oil field: area where large amounts of oil can be found underground

organic waste: also known as **biodegradable waste**, this is waste made of animal or plant matter that can be broken down by bacteria

outpost: isolated settlement

persecution: to be treated badly because of religion, race or political beliefs

petroleum: unrefined oil, also known as **crude oil**

polyester: man-made fabric made of **polyethylene**

polyethylene: type of plastic

port: a town or city with a harbour, or the left hand side of a ship (the right hand side is called **starboard**)

precarious: unstable or unbalanced

processing plant: place where raw materials are split into their component parts or turned into a product

protagonist: the main character of a drama, film or book

province: part of a country

quarterdeck: part of a ship's upper deck that runs from the centre to the **stern**

quay: a platform lying alongside or projecting into water for loading and unloading ships

quayside: a **quay** and the area around it

raw materials: basic material from which a product is made

reconnaissance: survey or research to find out information

recycle: to convert waste products into useable materials

refinery: a **processing plant** where raw materials are split into their component parts

refugee: person who leaves their home country to live in another country due to war or **persecution**

relegate: to assign a person an inferior job, or to become diminished in stature and importance

reservoir: a place where liquid is contained

retailer: people and places that sell things, such as shops or market traders

revolution: when citizens overthrow the government so they can change the way the country is run

run aground: when a vessel becomes immobilised due to hitting a raised area of river or ocean bed or enters water that is too shallow

rural: characteristic of the countryside

scapegoat: a person who is blamed for the wrongdoing or mistakes of others

scour: to scrub an object with rough material for cleaning purposes

seamstress: woman who sews as a job

sector: a particular part of an economy, society or area of professional activity

Serengeti: a geographical region of Africa where wildlife such as lions, zebras and elephants can be found

sheikh: an Arab leader, the head of a tribe, family or village

sheikhdom: an area of land under the control of a **sheikh**

ship breaking zone: place where old and unused ships are taken apart

shipping container: a standard sized metal container used for moving and shipping cargo and goods

shrewd: clever and a bit crafty

starboard: right hand side of a ship (the left hand side is called **port**)

stern: the back of a ship

subsidy: buying a part of, or giving money to a business or organisation to keep it going

sulphur: a chemical used to make matches, gunpowder and in medicine

sulphurous: something that contains sulphur

superstition: irrational belief in supernatural influences such as good or bad luck

superstructure: the visible part of a building or vessel

synthetic fibre: strand of material created by forcing fibre forming materials through holes (also see **artificial fibre**)

taxi-brousse: a mode of transport that is a cross between a taxi and a bus

trader: person who sells products

trawler: fishing boat used for **trawling**

trawling: to fish or catch with a trawl net

tribe: social division in a traditional society made up of connected families or communities

tuk-tuk: three-wheeled car used as a taxi in India

twenty foot equivalent unit (TEU): 20 foot long shipping container

Ultra Large Crude Carriers (ULCC): oil tanker that can carry 320,000-549,000 tonnes of oil

unindustrialised (less-developed) countries: a comparatively poor country with a less-developed social, industrial and economic structure

United Nations: an international organisation that monitors worldwide laws and security, social progress and human rights

Very Large Crude Carriers (VLCC): oil tanker that can carry 160,000-319,000 tonnes of oil

viscous: thick

wharf (wharves): level **quayside** where boats can be moored to load or unload goods

whipping boy: a young boy assigned to a prince or noble who is punished when his counterpart misbehaves, often used **metaphorically** to describe a **scapegoat**

wholesaler: person or company that sells goods in **bulk**, often to **retailers**

World Trade Organisation (WTO): an organisation that monitors world trade and attempts to make sure trade agreements are fair

yarn: thread used for knitting and weaving

Index

Further Information

Books

Fast Food Nation: What The All-American Meal is Doing to the World
Eric Schlosser (Penguin, 2002)

Globalization: A Very Short Introduction
Manfred B. Steger (Oxford University Press, 2009)

No Logo (Special Edition)
Naomi Klein (Fourth Estate, 10th Anniversary Edition, 2010)

Not On the Label: What Really Goes into the Food on Your Plate
Felicity Lawrence (Penguin, 2004)

The End of Poverty: How We Can Make it Happen in Our Lifetime
Jeffrey Sachs (Penguin, 2005)

184

Websites

Duck Spotting
beachcombersalert.org

Fairtrade Foundation
www.fairtrade.org.uk

Make Poverty History
www.makepovertyhistory.org

Trade Justice Movement
www.tjm.org.uk

Winter Sports in Dubai
www.skidxb.com

DVDs

An Inconvenient Truth
Al Gore and Davis Guggenheim (Paramount, 2006)

The Corporation
Mark Achbar (In 2 Film, 2006)